Other Books From Bolero Bird

Naive Melody: The Early Novellas of Michael Whone (2025)

Mind the Bits: Notes of a Schizophrenic - Michael Whone (2025)

little bit die - Jason Emde (2023)

Analysand

A Novel in Three Novelettes
Michael Whone

Bolero Bird edition 2025
Copyright © 2025 Michael Whone
All Rights Reserved

Analysand © 2025

Library and Archives of Canada
Whone, Michael
Analysand / Michael Whone
Formerly titled: Lo-Fi
Bolero Bird 1st Edition
ISBN: 978-1-0695067-1-9

Book Design by River Van Style

www.bolerobird.ca

Analysand

A Novel in Three Novelettes

Michael Whone

Visions
of
Johanna

Visions of Johanna

LONELY AS ALWAYS, EILEEN HAD been on my mind halfway through December. Devil had forbidden, she still defeated the cancer around her grown woman nipples. God had forbidden that we all contracted syphilis, the Nerds and I, and a few others not-so-innocently involved.

Reading Ayn Rand during the last weeks of December had been wonderful, especially since wondering if it was just as fair not feeling anything before I had placed the metaphorical shitty sock in my mouth with the *grown woman nipples* comment to Eileen—on top of Eileen's Fibromyalgia issues in bed and my consequent lasting lack of confidence. With my shitty foot symbolically in my mouth (only an empty verbal blunder that I had made) I still felt—as I read deeper into the layers of Ayn Rand's *The Virtue of Selfishness*—that I was being brainwashed.

In the summer following, Stefi assured me I was wrong about all of it. "You have an amazing life!" she said to me. And although she was comforting, I thought of her as somewhat of a grifting magpie. Nothing wrong with that, to her. I just prefer swooping cardinals.

Childhood memories were disappearing. "Buddha bought a beat-ah," they told me. "World War III is gonna end it all one day," the pip-squeak-peons I went to Kindergarten with told me, directly from the mouths of their fathers, I nearly undoubtedly thought. And as I thought of the psychotherapy I'd had leading up to December, none of it mattered. I felt a light mist in my head, pouring, beautifully, wildly ecstatic and incessantly so.

Let it all wash away down the toilet. And after all, despite my loneliness, *a flush beats a full house*. In poker hands that's not true, but my mom used to say that jokingly when I was a child, playing 500 with her and my dad. "One day you'll get it," she said. It's certainly true when you're living in a Toronto rooming house. She grew up in a small Scarborough townhouse with three brothers and a sister, although it could be just the hereditary schizophrenia talking. She wasn't a winning poker player whenever we played. Could have just been the rum and gin my parents shared as we played.

Near the end of the chapter near the end of the book, I put the book down to send Bob a message.

"I've been reading Ayn Rand."

He didn't take long, "Oh how's that going?" he asked.

"It's strange, I feel like a lot of it is just common sense. But I get the feeling, since she's a respected writer, that a lot of women had wrong ideas about this book back in the day. Like, it's all addressed to men, and all the undesirable social things men do, but really, I think it was meant as a commentary on both men and women equally. And because it looks like a pile of all the horrid things that men do, women become over-confident. Seeing as how I don't really do a lot of those things, it kind of made me feel confident. You should read it."

"What's it called?"

"The Virtue of Selfishness."

I explained the title a bit, since it comes off as a book-length cheat sheet for getting away with your narcissism. Blame men to absolve your own dysfunctions.

"Every time I read Ayn Rand I feel like I'm being brainwashed for some reason."

"I know the feeling," he said, surprising me a little. Bob's uninterested most of the time. You know, unless women are involved—early 20th century philosophers not included.

"Ya, I mean, I felt the same way when I read Anthem. That book is short, so is The Virtue of Selfishness, damn, I don't know what my mind would be like if I put some time into reading something like The Fountainhead. I think my mind would turn into a giant rain puddle for months."

He didn't respond for a while. I stretched out on my bed and felt a pleasant solitude.

My phone made a sound when Bob replied.

"How are you these days?"

"Just trying not to talk too much about other people, and assume things, you know? I feel great though. I feel like a huge weight has been lifted off of my shoulders. You know, I can't thank you enough for last winter. It meant a lot to me that you came over and said what you said. I thought a lot about that moment when you picked up the Sylvia Plath in my room."

"Lol," he wrote. "It's an epic book. Did you read it?"

"I did."

"Feel any better?"

"I don't want to say too much about other people, remember. The criticism is tough."

"I know. My two lesbian moms are asking for me. I should go, lest I be judged."

I finished stretching out.

Moments later, I received a message from Megan. I had talked with her one night at O'Reilly's. It was a private invite to a party on New Year's. I looked at the list of people going. None of the guys from the band were invited. It was mostly women on the invite list.

The strange thing about it wasn't the glorious amount of women attending the same party as me, or that they're all semi-famous musicians, it was that I had met most of them before (almost in some sort of past life), and because I knew all those people had lots of parties, but hadn't been invited before.

The following evening, I received another notification from the manager of Nerds. It was an invite to an East Coast tour on their tour bus. Hell, I'd known all these guys for years, mostly nothing doing and now what, they want me to be a roadie?

So I guess taking a few art classes and designing a few posters, and dropping a few leads to the promotors on the strip about RV sales guys I met, and suddenly the cat droppings, dirty sheets, stacks of sticky man-zines, spyware-infested screen at 2%, two full hampers in the corner, broken washing machine in the four-and-a-half foot high crawl space downstairs, bong resin-laden, ashen-screened pipe, and the screaming and yelling Chinese lady who is probably frying three-stoves-full of fresh cod, didn't seem so bad. Lella came upstairs afterwards and offered me an entire fish.

"No thanks," I said.

Mid-October was the start of my detox from alcohol, caffeine, and unhealthy food, consequently the start of an improved attitude. I still wander occasionally, pining—not for women, but for anything—a place to be, a connection, a glimpse, some sort of flicker, seeking something within the thin sheet of my field of vision. The plaza near the university, the strip, O'Reilly's, the fried chicken joint, beer stores, streetcars, and the familiar places where

I wandered: all these became less doused in indulgent, alcoholic memories, and gradually new architecture emerged in those places, new façades had only revealed themselves in my mind.

When Megan invited me to a party on New Year's Eve with members of some of the city's best music acts, I felt like I was breaking free, breaking in, but not breaking at all. I didn't really go to the party. I went but didn't go in, passed by only in happenstance, but for some reason I stood on Megan's porch talking to her at 2 AM on the first morning of the year, and everything seemed different.

"I've been thinking about you," she said.

"What were you thinking?"

"Just how you were doing. I've been peppered with thoughts, some of them good. I think you're different, and there's something special about you."

She laughed, a nervous laugh that seemed a little too tactful to be genuine, a laugh that remained characteristically unchanged since the first time we spoke. I wasn't sure what to make of it.

We had only one previous conversation and that was two years ago at O'Reilly's. She had expressed deep gratitude for the love that manifested between herself and the guitarist in Nerds, gratitude for the ability to reveal her true character to him while feeling she had always been mostly elusive to other people.

I hadn't thought about her much in the passing years, but as we stood there on her porch, she seemed to be exactly herself, that her manner reciprocated my trepidation and diffidence.

"Thank you so much," I said in a revering tone, "You're so nice. You're really nice."

"But I'm a lot more than that."

I wouldn't doubt it, I thought.

In a glimpse through the thin plane, I saw Little Hollywood

sitting on my face in the lane between Megan's house and the one next-door. *Strange*, I thought.

I had spent the summer running around with a young woman named Johanna. Little Hollywood is her sister. Megan and her boyfriend Ted spotted Johanna and me together three of four times throughout the summer.

But Little Hollywood is a heavy-set, and top-heavy young woman, a little more than a year older than her sister. I guess that the extra weight has more to do with her Olanzapine prescription than her lifestyle. If Little Hollywood wasn't on anti-psychotics and mood stabilizers, she probably would be ample and cherub-like, matching her pale, angelic face. However, her figure hasn't stifled the sexual emancipation she found for herself, and in years passing, I've learned she's extremely intelligent, and usually the funniest person I know. Problem being: every ten minutes spent with Little Hollywood requires about thirty minutes of studying Urban Dictionary afterwards, to (still only slightly) comprehend what in the heck she's saying.

Ted, Megan's boyfriend, is a guitarist in Nerds, a new rock and roll band that's on a few independent music charts. I've known him for almost ten years. In fact, I've known everyone in that band for almost ten years—except the singer. Ted was likely waiting upstairs for Megan.

On the subject of Little Hollywood's anti-psychotics and mood stabilizers, Olanzapine (commonly known as Zyprexa) inhibits certain functions of the brain. I'm far from an expert on the subject of this medication, but what I do know is: people have the ability to see several aspects of a given situation, sort of like analyzing a mix-tape with only one song repeated again and again. Maybe *Stairway to Heaven*, for instance. First, they hear what they think the song could be about, then the song ends, and it starts again as the next, and next, and next songs on the mix-tape. Perhaps they think their initial interpretation could be wrong, and continue to dissect the lyrics each time the song repeats to examine every possible meaning. People with anxiety, mild psychotic thought behaviours, and the like, do such things in almost every situation they're in, sometimes *while being involved* in a social situation that requires their attention. Unfortunately, the complexity of a situation leaves them unable to focus socially, and end up not really seeing every aspect of a situation, and then filter meaning to suit a given bias they'd like to see (because it's easier), and the lack of focus when participating in social situations often leaves them more wary of the situation than they should be. This accurately describes the experiences I've had with Little Hollywood.

Stairway to Heaven is the perfect song to describe people who suffer from such thought patterns, because it's a pretty song for the most part, but suddenly turns distorted near the end. Often people don't know where their distorted thoughts came from, but it's not easy to resolve such distorted thought patterns, though the supposedly appropriate medications are supposed to inhibit the brain function that allows our thoughts to become self-abusive (distorted).

The problem is: medication like Zyprexa doesn't help. Most of these thoughts in young people came from questions of sexuality, religion, ethnicity, body image issues, and other imposed social realities. Meaning: a medication like Zyprexa, which causes severe weight gain (think Christian Bale as Dick Cheney) puts a person in a position where a psychiatrist is telling the patient to take the medication, and failure to take it will result in being locked up in a psychiatric hospital, but at the same time, the patient encounters her General Practitioner telling her ominously, "You could die," from the medications and excessive weight gain caused from it. Yet, the patient trusts both doctors.

Megan flicked her ash over the porch steps to my side while simultaneously making a shoo-shoo gesture.

"Okay, okay! I was just leaving. I didn't mean to come here anyway. Thank you for the invite but I wasn't going to come. I don't really belong here. I was headed home."

"Where's home?"

"Bloor West. This is on my route. I went to the bar and had my first beer of the year just after midnight with Pat," I said. Pat Murray is a music promoter, and social activist know-it-all. Undoubtedly everyone at Megan's party knows him. "I read most of the day and slept until just before the countdown and I didn't get to the bar until last call. I was walking home and I forgot that it was night time. I don't like walking through the park at night so I was deciding if I should turn around or walk up to Parkside and turn back around onto Westminster, over to—"

"Indian."

"Yeah, Indian. That's my route."

"I don't like walking down Queen past Dufferin, definitely not past Ossington, and there's no chance in hell I'm walking on The Queensway. I don't even like walking on Parkside, but on the Queensway there's a good chance—"

"Someone might swerve off the road. Yeah, there's a lot of young men who aren't very smart about their driving, particularly on a night like this."

It's a conflict of interest. My past. Her past. My guilt. Her grief. In fact, almost everyone has had an incident with a car accident, usually traumatic, and I remembered another thing we spoke about at O'Reilly's the time we met: her late father.

A tall young woman with blue eyes and dyed black hair came out onto the front porch and said, "Megan, who's this?" Megan was taking a drag.

"I was just leaving," I said, looking off into the distance out toward the park as drops from the eave flitted down on my eye.

"Who you talking to?" Megan said.

"Oh, sorry. I just had a bit of snow on my eyelashes."

Shawn came outside next.

The evening was mild, upholding a light drizzle. It was a good time to leave.

"Shawn, good to see you again," I said and we shook hands.

"If this rain went away it would be perfect for a longboard rip," he said.

Mid-December, I saw Shawn on the strip. *You know you're having a good winter when you're longboarding in January*, was the last thing I said to him.

"Better go now," I said.

It wasn't difficult to find my way back up to Bloor—a different story after four or five pints at one of the shows on the strip. And if any time I've lost myself staggering home, it is certain that I was looking for something, anything other than Bloor Street. There have been a few times I've wondered if the intensity of longing for an object of affection can be directly connected to the number of pints I've had before leaving a bar alone. Pining. Pints. Sounds similar. Doubtlessly the thoughts of a drunk. I've discerned that discernment eludes drunks.

The last moments with Eileen remained vivid, moments after trying to love her seemed noteworthy. I felt, for once, a woman was able to relate to me without reducing me to a drunken buffoon. She didn't need to—confident about who and where she was in her own right—Eileen's mind was healthy, and it impressed me. I think she knew the place I was in, yet could not cease loving like a healthy woman, which the slideshow in my mind, as I approached the Circle K, played back like the journal of a mother concerned for a wayward son.

We sat together listening to the folk music acts at one of the quirky, trendy, retro diner cafés on the strip. She held onto me all night. We held hands and she caressed my leg. My face was flush and it was difficult to focus on the songs. She made love no different. She was the most sensual woman I have ever been with. It seemed unfair to me that every other woman I'd been with had taken me for granted—enter Eileen—and I treated her the way every other woman had treated me, because I had become a fed up, hopeless, lowly alcoholic burn out.

It has been good to look back on my time with Eileen as a first glimpse of a relationship that seemed like a workwithable idea. I ruined it, but Eileen's influence remained positive knowing that she could be the last woman I fuck to try to make my pain go away. And it was obvious to me, the way I tried to make love, that I could never appreciate her unless I was healthy.

"Ugh! I stepped in shit," I said to Eileen.

"Oh, I'm sorry. Turn the light on."

When I met her she was looking to adopt a German Shepherd for her daughter. At first, when Eileen brought the puppy into their apartment at the beginning of October, it was her nearly-teenage daughter's responsibility to walk the dog before bed time. Midway through November, the list of duties to care for the dog had somehow made way onto Eileen's already infinite todo list.

"Do you think she even took him out?"

"Oh ya, she did. Here." Eileen wiped my foot with paper towel and started wiping up the dog shit on the kitchen floor. "Sorry," she said.

"Can I have one of these peanut butter banana cookies? Or are they for school tomorrow?"

"No, you can't have those."

"Oh, it's okay, I'll get something at Circle K. I like to get a coffee when I go on my route. I actually enjoy the walk home."

After our love making (although it's difficult to call it that) we discussed whether I should sleep over. She had to be at work in less than five hours, and she had warned me that men have had trouble sleeping beside her, a subject of conversation that was mentioned before the first time we made love. I decided it was best that she had proper sleep before work.

We kissed goodbye and I made my way up Indian over to Bloor, and into the Circle K for a coffee. That was the last time I saw Eileen.

Walking into Circle K on New Year's Eve, I remembered I quit drinking regular coffee, so I walked through the convenience store aimlessly and confused. The final night I was with Eileen I was still drinking caffeinated coffee. The same clerk was on duty.

"There's coffee," the clerk said, pointing to the containers in the corner.

"Do you have decaf?" I didn't know what else to say. I didn't know what I wanted. Something they didn't have.

"Sorry," he said, looking towards the corner. "No."

There was a bit of magic to the way I met Eileen.

It was the beginning of September, 2018, and it was the start of another college year for me. I wasn't enthusiastic about studying art for another year, particularly because of the feeling that art theory, rudiments, and practicum ruin the mythology of the creation. At least for me.

I missed my first class of the year. I missed my second class of the year. I missed my third class of the year. As the second week of the semester was approaching, I received a phone call from a marketing company I had applied to in the summer.

In my first week back on campus for my second year, there was a woman doing administrative work at the front door to one of the main arts buildings. She hadn't been there in my first year, but I recognized her immediately, although didn't know her well. She was the mother of Martin French, one of the concert promoters at O'Reilly's on the strip. Martin was a doorman when I went there one night with the bass player in Nerds. Martin and I became friends and obviously he had introduced me to his mother.

I re-introduced myself to Martin's mom there at the university and we started a conversation. Many busy people went in and out of the art building, so we only spoke for a few minutes, then I sat at a couch near some of the tables in one of the common rooms. Soon, Martin's mom sat at a table nearby, eating her lunch, and we continued our conversation. I mentioned that I had hoped Martin would ask me to do some designs for O'Reilly's.

We laughed at a few memes she showed me as she ate her salad and in just a few minutes after starting back at her post, Martin contacted me with my first poster assignment. Over the next few weeks, I designed several posters for the bar. The bands were impressed with a few of the posters, some of them were just acceptable, and some were rejected by the bands. Normal fare.

The posters for O'Reilly's was my body of work—meager at that—and I went into the company for my interview on the last day to withdraw from university. The creative director asked me a few questions, and on the spot, she offered me a position. I struggled to decide if going into the work world, leaving university behind was best.

I visited the psychotherapist that day, to see if she could help me come to a best possible decision about leaving, or staying in university. I sat in the psychotherapist's lobby, waiting, but I left before she saw me. I knew, there, what I would do.

The first year of my degree had been tough. As an older student I struggled to fit in with mostly teenage students, particularly young women. I wished the young women I met there took the initiative to honestly express their motives. They seemed horny, couldn't express it, and in turn conversations with them had malicious overtones. Maybe I'm wrong, but whatever the case, I wasn't ready for another year of teen angst and unconscious, sexually motivated passive-aggressiveness.

I left campus thinking I was ready for that next great part of my life—nothing as psychedelic as my past, but something sobering, and honestly rewarding.

In those first weeks back at the university for another year, quitting all of my nasty vices seemed like the only option, and working in art, where I felt a certain belonging, helped me muster the confidence I needed to follow through with cleaning up. That's what I did, and at my new job, I finally had somewhere to go, something to do, a purpose. I thought I felt great.

I wore hip clothes all around the strip, with a fantastic haircut and a few different options for nice shoes to choose from. People looked at me. I don't know what they were thinking when they were looking but I liked it. I took a few pictures of myself and put them on Tinder.

First I met Nadine. She was a polyamorist with a husband, two kids, worked as a medical lab technician, had a pretty smile, a sexy hourglass figure, and bright blue, seductive eyes. I met Nadine for the first time on my birthday. She was almost ten years older and started off a little shy, but as we talked she opened up and her inner vixen became prominent.

"I used to smoke More's," she said. "They were the most sophisticated cigarette."

More cigarettes were a long, thin cigarette, 100s they were called, and aren't available anymore. The tobacco was wrapped in a brown paper and had a golden coloured filter, and only came in 20-packs. I can't remember exactly when *More* cigarettes went off the market, but high end cigarettes were all under six dollars a pack back then.

"It's funny: such a disgusting habit, but some cigarettes look really classy. I remember More. More's? I liked those."

Our conversation was attempting to feel out any apprehension we may have had about what was a noticeable age gap between us. She may have been older than she said.

"I used to be so cool. I'm not that classy anymore," she said.

"Ya, me neither. More's were the perfect cigarette to hold in one hand, while there's and Olde English 40 in the other. On one hand you're trashy, and on the other hand you're totally classy. It balances everything out, right? It's like trashy chic. That's an actual style. I think I've heard of it."

We laughed and she started to blush.

We talked comfortably to each other, fluid and entertaining for both of us for almost two hours over coffee in Starbucks.

Putting on my jacket, as we were leaving, she waited for me at the door. I turned around, facing her, facing me near the door. So sexy. Incredibly so.

"What are you doing now," I asked her.

"I'm just going home to get everything ready for the apartment tomorrow."

She had an Airbnb apartment in her basement. Every day after working at the lab she did housekeeping when the guests checked out.

"Well, I don't drive. I don't need a ride or anything, I just felt like savouring this moment as much as I can because I really like you."

"You're cute," she said. "This is my car."

I hugged her, and I felt like it might have been a waste of time for her if I didn't kiss her—but that's besides the point—hardly anyone ever called me cute, not on a first date. I kissed her on the cheek but her wavy, dyed red hair covered her face and I felt awkward for a moment.

"That's it?" she said.

I looked straight into her eyes for a short moment and kissed her. Twice. I don't remember what we said after, but whatever it was, we were like giddy school children that had just tried cotton candy for the first time.

Wow, I thought.

I walked to the streetcar stop and I felt elated. I got on the streetcar and I still felt elated. I looked at my phone and saw that I had a new Tinder match. It was Eileen, and that felt even better.

I rode the streetcar to O'Reilly's because Martin put me on the VIP list for my birthday. The bartender had a drink ready for me as soon as I walked in the door, a gift from Martin.

"I don't think I can stay here too long," I said to Martin. "I just had a date. We had a little kiss and everything. This—" I pointed at the stage. "This is too much right now. I need a distraction, but this is too much."

I saw Martin at O'Reilly's a few days later. He did most of his business at the bar, if not, online with co-workers and bands from out of town. At the bar, he was usually with someone.

He was with the other man.

And the other man. And the other man.

And the other man, one of Johanna's roommates, who I had run into on the strip just before I arrived. Neither of us had any plans, which of course is always a perfect time to see who's in O'Reilly's, so we walked in together.

Everyone knows the other man is the bass player in Nerds. He's about six feet tall, lanky, but carries a little extra weight in the mid-section, hair thinning as thirty is approaching. I've always known him as a very knowledgeable musician and music buff. The day I met him he flawlessly played Jaco Pastorius' *Portrait of Tracy* on his bass. We often discuss a mutual desire to hear *The Rite of Spring* performed someday, a conversation that usually concludes with a toast to *good music without dancers and dancing, and therefore no ballerino codpieces.*

The other man was also there, the drummer in Nerds. He has a cute blonde-haired girlfriend that no one has ever seen, except in pictures of the two of them on cruises, and in cars on streets with slick architecture none of us recognize. He doesn't drink much, takes Public Transit, yet, everyone talks like he's got money somewhere, somehow. I think it has to do with the way he dresses. He always seems to look like a young Bruce Cockburn, with a dull coloured suit, red pants (always red), thin tie, and shiny hair that doesn't yet seem to have a touch of grey, even in his late twenties. There's rumours that he's a voice-over actor in some Anime cartoon that hasn't been sold to American television companies yet. And some people say he doesn't do voice-overs at all. He's actually in a television show in Japan, in which every character is played by him, the other man.

The other man is over fifty and has been a musical mainstay in Toronto for almost as long as I've been living. I don't want to incriminate such a beautiful man for something I have known absolutely nothing about at this point in my life or any, but his hands were shaking when he said hello to me, reaching out to shake mine, his eyes were twitching a little, and I'd like to make a reference to billiards and black balls, but I think that's a little over the top given the circumstances. He lives with his ex-wife, and most times has at least one of a about a dozen little pixie girlfriends orbiting him when he's at a show. It was the first time he said hello to me.

The other man and I walked into the bar together. He's a few inches over six feet tall, is insecure about being underweight. That is, he eats anything he can to gain weight, but looks as thin as a 90s supermodel and drunk women shout, "You're hot!" at him when he walks down the strip after last call. He does himself up to appeal to both men and women, with long black hair, black fingernails, and he has hazel eyes but wears two colours of blue contact lenses. He plays a six string bass in a band that's on hiatus because they're going for a more Nine Inch Nails type sound.

The other man is an inch under six feet tall, has a haircut that's on par, if not, better than the other man, is lanky but carries some extra weight in the mid-section, has long fingernails on his right hand from years of classical guitar performance, but doesn't use them because he hasn't played for anyone, including himself, in almost five years. He's wearing a $200 denim jacket over top of a black and white baseball tee that has a graphic of a pyramid and illuminati, burgundy skinny jeans that show off his firm thighs, and Doc Marten's that rise above the ankles.

I'm Ox in the illuminati t-shirt: sort of a minor-league junkball pitcher of sorts, who isn't allowed on the team coach for smoking too many Bull Durhams and snoring, an ex-guitarist with a sound a little like Charlie Byrd, and probably the best knowledge of music theory at this table, a knowledge that never made me much money with music, but now, mid-thirties—although I don't play music anymore—I could possibly make a go of it because of my connections to one of the major venues on the strip.

Martin scooted over when his girlfriend Shell arrived so she could sit beside him, across the table from me. Shell is about six feet tall above some short heels, has different colours of layered hair parted in the middle, and legs long and slender enough to look like they've been altered in Photoshop. Her voice is deep and sultry, and no one knows what her best feature is. Maybe her eyes, but as for my concern, it's her lips. Almost painfully vexing to look at. Like heat waves on a car roof in the summer. Like looking at a tangible definition of how the dew point on the hottest day of the year makes anything bearable.

"I just bought some Wes pants," I told Johanna in a text message. I had bought new burgundy pants earlier in the day, pants somewhat like the red skinny jeans Wes always wears. I took a picture of Wes sitting at the table beside ours in his trademark red jeans and sent it to Johanna.

A few minutes later she responded, "Red?"

"You know it! Have you written anything lately?"

"Ugh! I haven't been able to write anything lately. Have you started Desolation Angels yet?"

I had been looking for a used copy of *Desolation Angels* for years. I had only seen it in bookstores when I had no money to buy it and frowned at the thought of ordering it online.

When I was in the used bookstore with Johanna in the summer, I mentioned I was looking for it. Later in the fall, a few weeks after Eileen ended things, I met up with Johanna at the bookstore and found it. Finding it was magical to me, recalling that the last time we went there I told her I had been trying to find it for several years.

I wrote back to her, "I read the Preface."

She didn't respond.

I had read the Preface Joyce Johnson wrote denigrating Kerouac and his bitter attitude towards the world at that time in his life.

"And just like that I fell out of love with Jack Kerouac. If Kerouac died and became a woman, he'd be writing books called Heart Shaped Dildo. Still, there is something in his writing that captured me for many years, something I've observed. There are certain conditions placed on women that men often do not understand, and for me, if women could participate fully and carefree in any circumstance with men, I wouldn't be reading Joan Didion, Ayn Rand, and Jennifer Egan all week.

"If I can't be with an intelligent woman in real life, I'll pretend to be while I'm lying on my bed, so to speak.

"Lol."

She didn't respond until 4 in the morning. "I've never read any Kerouac. I want to though," she wrote.

THE ACQUAINTANCES (NERDS, MUSIC HORDES, et. al.) of the summer of 2018 had drifted from my thoughts, aside from the relationship with Johanna. I met all of these people at O'Reilly's within the last ten years, and although our relationship began under the guise of alcoholism, her presence and friendship had been great.

I like to tell stories and Johanna says she does too. I enjoy incredibly mundane stories so boring that there is no other way to respond than laugh at the absurdity of telling such nonsense in the first place.

Sitting in a park in her neighbourhood, The Beaches, one Day in July, looking out onto the lake, I asked her, "Tell me a story from your childhood."

"Like what?"

"I don't know, just something you remember. Did you ever go to the park when you were a kid?"

"Ya."

"Well, do you have any memories at the park?"

She laughed.

"Ya. I have a memory of a seagull stealing my hotdog. My dad bought us hotdogs one day. Everything was normal, and I was eating a hotdog, and then it was gone. A seagull took it right out of my mouth."

I laughed.

"Oh my God! Ya, seagulls are little shits. That happened to me once too. It wasn't that long ago, though. I remember I bought a donut at Tim Hortons one day and I probably had like just enough to buy it, and I walked out eating it. I didn't make it past the drive-thru before the seagull came down and took it right out of my hand."

We laughed.

"I wanted to yell at it, like: Who do you think I am? Some kind of bitch? Go find a trash can or something! When was that? That wasn't that long ago," I said.

"I think everyone probably has a story like that."

"It's just funny that a little girl—how old were you?"

I was going to say, I think it's funny that a little girl was just having a nice day, a wonderful memory with her dad, and a seagull came along and snatched it from her hands.

"I don't know. Maybe eight or nine."

"Did you cry?"

"I don't remember."

"I'm just imagining this little girl with a hotdog, all happy, nice day at the beach with her parents, everything's going swell, then this bird snatches it and she just starts sobbing."

She didn't laugh but I did. We both had a taste for existential scenarios like this. You know, the metaphorical hotdog being appropriated from the flimsy grasp. She had a copy of *Being and Nothingness* in her room, hadn't read it—no time to—but she was obsessed with *Lolita*. She even wore a low-cut, sleeveless, *Lolita* shirt that showed her midriff, usually paired with a black or plaid skirt.

She was in her early twenties and I was approaching thirty-five. The man she felt romantic about was also my age.

We walked back into town and she spotted an old 60s T-Bird parked at the sidewalk. It was sky blue, with the top down. We stood there admiring it. Thunderbirds were never much my favourite. I always had the thought that The Beach Boys kind of ruined their mystique. I mean, beggars can't be choosers, but I've always been more of a Corvette guy, if we were talking 60s cars.

"Is this your car?" some guy said to either Johanna or me.

"No," I said. "We were just looking at it."

"It looks like it's in good condition. You know what kind of car it is?" he asked, like he didn't know. Incredibly strange for a man his age.

"I think it's a T-Bird. The seats are kind of cracking a little."

"Oh ya. For the age it's holding up pretty nice."

"Could be the original paint."

Johanna just stood there. I'm not sure the guy was admiring the car as much as he was admiring Johanna. I didn't tell Johanna that I didn't really like T-Birds that much but she told me another story, walking back to her place.

"My dad said he was going to buy me an old car like that, one time."

"What happened?"

"We were just driving and talking about old cars and he said he would buy me one. I don't know what happened but he just never did."

"Hmm."

The first time we met, she described her feelings of insecurity and brought them up a few other times as we were becoming friends, but as I came to know her I didn't see that quality in her. I felt mostly that she was intimidated by me and my ability to tell stories, like her stories were less important. But, I'm unable to tell it for her, and anyone else really, and sometimes the people who I wished would speak more and tell me more about themselves aren't willing to. Underneath somewhat of a guising lens of *I don't knows* there are some real stories in her mind to share, she hasn't figured out what relevance they have to her or others, or me, especially since by the end of the summer, when she was living with the man she was after, I hardly saw her.

I waited for the streetcar a few blocks from Johanna's house. Bob, one of the cooks at O'Reilly's was there. I've known him since he had just graduated high school.

O'Reilly's was a different place when I met Bob ten years ago through the guys who would be Nerds. As much as grinding it out, struggling to sober myself for almost a decade, the alcoholic in me and repeat offender of funneling quarts of Corona with bikini-wearing college girls from Québec faded nicely over the winter when Nerds planned to set out on their first tour. I wondered for a few seconds how I became involved, and then I didn't wonder anymore.

There's not much of a beginning to the story, absolutely no middle to it, but we left the bar before last call one night, headed out to another bar in Bob's car with one of the waitresses. The waitress got in the front, two guys in the back of his car and I was the last one to get in. He started to pull away before I finished drunkenly getting in the car and I did the splits with my right knee jamming onto the street. One of the guys yelled, "Bob!" and he stopped.

Heading into a university program to study literature after

high school, hopefully to be a writer some day, Bob was a golden boy. When I threatened to sue him, we made a settlement and he found his place cooking in restaurants. In ten fine years he was able to climb to second in command at a large restaurant with a very affluent client base.

I hardly ever saw him before I met Johanna. I asked him what he was doing there as I waited next to the T-Bird for the streetcar. He said, "I'm going to the gym."

"Oh, I thought I might ask you to go for a beer."

"I've got no money. Someone broke into my car and stole all my baseball equipment. I have to replace it before my game on Wednesday. It's going to cost me about $500."

"When did you start playing baseball?"

"Just recently. I'm trying to clean up."

"Ya, and you're going to the gym too, eh?"

"It's been about 139 days since I've had alcohol, and I quit smoking," he paused to think. "About three weeks ago."

"You don't do any drugs?" I said, like I was surprised.

"No. I smoke green, but I'm not going to be giving that up."

"Well, they say it's sacred. You know, like, New-Age hippy people, so I guess it can't be totally bad. I need to quit smoking cigarettes. And drinking. We should go for a beer sometime though. Oh. I guess you aren't drinking anymore."

He paused for a moment, looking for his car.

"Well, I guess I'll run into you at the bar," I said.

I waited for the streetcar, finishing a cigarette or two. Back home, alone in my bed, late in the afternoon, I had a notification on my phone.

It said:

YOU HAVE A MEMORY TO LOOK BACK ON TODAY
—Facebook

I looked at the memory, an old post I had written on Facebook exactly three years before.

A seagull just stole a donut from my hand.
—July 25, 2015

I told Johanna about the Facebook reminder of the stolen donut in a text message.

She said, "ahahahaha omg"

"Ya. That's weird," I replied.

"That timing though."

"Haha. OMG the synchronicity of my life. It's like you stalked me before this morning."

She didn't respond.

About a month later at O'Reilly's, having drinks at the bar with Bob late at night, I talked to him about a date I had been on with a woman in her early 50s. Aside from feeling noticeably destitute sitting at a table across from her, it was the best date I had ever been on.

We hit the peak of our date at a salad bar, 35 minutes in. As she was stabbing chunks of hard-boiled egg, I was trying to scrape more of the tiny bacon pieces onto my fork, and I brushed her foot with mine, leading us into some flirty footsies under the table, which wound down to nothing afterward. I took a bus back home to my loneliness and lack of enthusiasm.

Almost as soon as I sat down for a beer with Bob, before telling him about fine fifties footsies lady, I got a few messages from Tina. Bob knew of her.

Tina was a promoter at the bar. She asked me to go for coffee right away, and feeling elated, probably manic, I inexhaustibly sent her a load of nonsensical, drunk text messages. Turned out I found out later that she had a boyfriend anyway.

The Tinder match with Tina lasted less than two hours and that was the end of my summer dating. What was necessary was to earn some income.

The three of us, Bob, Aiden, and Sam, the attractive and well-dressed waitress sat in the bar after close.

Sam was behind the bar still cleaning after her shift and the conversation the four of us weren't having died, and died again, and again, like the moment chose to pulp itself into internally diminishing microcosms of death. I did what I could to revive the conversation from flatline.

"I'm not really a fan of stand-up comedy," I said. "People seem to like it, but I find most comedians kind of distasteful. Sometimes when you're being funny, it's too easy to say things you probably shouldn't. Like all kinds of racist and sexist stuff, ya know?"

"I think that's the point," Bob said.

"What do you mean it's the point?"

"No one's listening to comedians joke about the weather, comedians have grit."

Sam pretended to be intrigued by the conversation.

"You know who I like? This is a good example of what I mean. I like that guy. What's his name? I can't remember his name."

"Oh ya! That guy," Aiden said. "I know that guy."

I paused, looking around thinking of his name.

"Oh ya! Dave Chappelle. I like Dave Chappelle though. Have you guys ever seen the Chappelle show?"

With a combination of drunken, lethargic, grunt-like noises it was confirmed that they had seen it.

"Have you ever seen that episode where he's a black, blind, white supremacist? I thought that was one of his best. I said that to a sweet little black honey last year at the university. She said something like: 'White people always say that. It's a really stupid skit.'

"I just let her have her point because I didn't want to fire her up, but it's true. Like, if you were blind, you'd hear all the crap messages out there trying to undermine cultural diversity and gender equality and maybe you'd think that way too," I said.

Sam, the fiery waitress is a feminist, and also a favourite artist of mine in the city, album cover designer, and somewhat of an expert on popular music. I met her in my first year of university, we weren't close but I've been attracted to her for quite some time, she has a husband and kids, and my awkwardness in her presence is amusing for me to think about.

"My grandmother is blind," Aiden said. "And she's not racist."

Bob grunted.

I looked at Sam and shrugged my shoulders. Simply put, I was following suit. You know, a Jack-o-hearts-in-a-coffin.

Sam played Eddie Cochran's *Summertime Blues.*

"Feel like dancing Bob?"

He cracked a crooked smile. "Heh," slipped out.

I respect Bob. I respect him because he talks to everyone and treats everyone as equals. When he goes out to drink around the strip or up in Yorkville, he talks to anyone, even if he's just met them, like he'd been a close friend for years. I admire that.

In the winter past, as I was struggling in my first year of university, and none of my friends seemed to care when I told them on Facebook how awful I felt, nobody cared. Who would?

But Bob sent me a message.

A few weeks later he came to my house to give me an old turntable he'd stored in his basement. We sheltered ourselves from the sharp cold and flurries of February, hardly able to hold cigarettes in icy hands, sitting in my room listening to Captain Beefheart, Frank Zappa, and Miles Davis.

"You're reading The Bell Jar?" Bob asked.

It was a good question really because I had forgotten it was there.

"No, I've been reading Žižek. Have you read it?" I was still referring to Sylvia Plath.

"I think so."

"Was it any good?"

"I don't remember."

He picked it up, fanned all the way to the end and read, "Ever since I'd learned about the corruption of Buddy Willard my virginity weighed like a millstone around my neck. It had been of such enormous importance to me for so long that my habit was to defend it at all costs. I had been defending it for five years and I was sick of it."

"Whoa! What's that about?"

"It's about losing her virginity."

"The whole book?"

"I think so."

I had recalled that he wanted to be a writer a long time ago, and I found him as impressive then as when we first met.

He's a tall, thin ginger with a personality that could be described as strong and silent. But he lets loose and busts out of his shell sometimes, never repeating his stories, with plenty of new ones to tell at any time, and I think what I admire most is his ability to seem confident without being self-centered or over-confident. Vulnerable without being weak or timid, and participates without being too competitive. A true gentleman.

I had been living in a college dorm with four young women for a month. The first week of living there I snuck in an old girlfriend before the female housemates got back from winter vacation. I went a little crazy because every time I entered a common room alone with one of three of the four women, she'd turn around and present her back to me. The fourth woman, a large Mexican young woman, was in love with a tall, thin man who came over for her pizza she had delivered most nights.

The cute Colombian girl had all of her bags packed and drifted off into the cold darkness early one morning. She always said hi to me walking around the university campus after. I didn't understand what she said when she would continue the conversation but she had a big smile that was almost worth stopping for.

Before April, only one of the female housemates had been Canadian. I tried talking to her, she was a cute young artist, almost twenty, but most of her time in common areas of the house was spent convincing the large, young Mexican woman that her boyfriend loved her.

If she wasn't always consoling the large Mexican because her boyfriend only came over for Dominos, I would have spent all my time with the young Canadian woman and most of it would have been spent thinking about touching her taut, white, freckled skin and prairie blonde hair found at the edge of her earth, pristine and untouched, only to be windswept into criminally fragile moments for the wind, as she undressed in her room.

By the end of my lease in the house with the four young university students, just before the start of my second year of grad school, finally I heard the amorous sounds of the large, young Mexican girl making love to her boyfriend. I was happy for her.

When Eileen and I split, I met up with Johanna at a coffee shop, around the end of October, there was frost on the ground, wilting shrubs, frosty leaves, but everything was looking notably verdant, so to speak.

I was with Nadine, the polyamourist lab technician when marijuana was legalized, and I worried she'd hook up with all of the other men. I had a quarter of a peanut butter cup left from the past winter, which I ate, mostly with Alex, high on bong hits from his bong, in his room in the same dorm neighbourhood as I was living. I felt a demiurge on that monumental, verdant day with Nadine, that I don't feel often. So I ate a sliver of a peanut butter cup, ended up walking into a gas station, pouring myself a coffee, and walking out without paying. As I inadvertently stole a coffee, something I wrote in a text message conversation struck Nadine as odd, and remained problematic for her in the remaining ten to twelve days we shared in *It's Complicated* status.

Nadine and I went to Dollarama on Spadina and Adelaide after what would be our last date, which so happened to be at Hooters. I forgot what either Nadine or I was looking for in Dollarama, but I saw Pat Murray there. "They're out of Milk Duds," Pat said, with a few larger-than-normal white floaties in his blue eyes, and I looked at him puzzled for a few seconds, then I just laughed. Apparently milk duds are *his* ritual. "He's baked as fuck!" I said to Nadine when he walked away to find some kind of semi-satiating substitute.

Across the street from the Dollarama was the coffee shop I sat in with Johanna "I have to hand write a chapter for this guy," Johanna said.

"Why would you do that?" I asked.

"He said he wants this part to look like handwritten letters."

"How long is it?"

"I don't know. Like 7 pages."

"I hope he's paying you for that. Don't do stuff like that for free."

"He is. Fifty dollars."

"Okay, that's not bad," I said.

She was killing me on the poster gig. Everyone wanted her posters and I was just running around putting them up. I was happy for her that she was earning some money finally, after a summer that had been financially unstable for her.

"How's things with ... what's her name?" she asked

"Eileen?"

"Ya."

"Mmm," I said. "There was a problem with the physical chemistry."

She didn't say anything about that. A few weeks later Johanna was in a relationship with the man she was enamored by, the man I inadvertently helped primp her confidence to pursue all throughout the summer.

"I can't get myself to do the work," she said.

"You'll get it finished. Just think of the money. You want the money, right?"

"Ya!"

"Well, don't talk to me until it's done," I told her, and left.

Bob was sitting at a table in the same coffee shop a few weeks later, reading. Johanna in the same window as a couple of weeks before, in the same seat where she was handwriting those letters. She still hadn't finished them. I ignored Johanna because I could see she was writing.

I sat with Bob and he put his book in his backpack. "What are you—what were you reading?" I asked.

"It's a book about addiction."

"Why are you reading that?"

"Because I want to get clean."

I tried to be careful with my words, and stumbled a bit on how to say this to him without being offensive, but I said, "You aren't in any trouble, are you?"

"I'm a lot better now."

"Were you doing anything Nefarious?"

"I've quit drinking and smoking. Last weekend I just went to Popeyes and ordered fifty dollars worth of chicken there."

"I like Popeyes. Were you having friends over?"

"No. It was for me. I ate the whole thing."

"Why would you do that?"

"I was baked as fuck," he said in a flushed voice, looked pensive for a second and then sighed. I winced a little when his brothy breath hit me.

We continued talking about addictions—drugs, sex, food, drinks, all of that. I was convinced clean was the way things had to go. I tried to convince him to write more, about the whole experience of breaking free— something I had taken up when I was working at a coffee shop, producing art in university, smoking bongs with Alex, my artist friend at the university, and neighbour next to my place when I was writing a novella living in that college dormitory with the four young, female undergrads.

The summer came, the Columbian woman had gone, the young female artist was bound for home near Niagara Falls, and the short, feisty South Asian woman may have still been waiting for me in her bed on the first floor. However, not likely, because I couldn't hear the song *Despacito* coming from her room after I moved out.

I ran into Bob on the strip, sometime in the middle of summer, just after the failed release of my novella, and he told me he couldn't talk because he had to work.

"You're always working, eh?" I asked.

"Ya, one of these days I'm just going to quit my job and go to Europe."

"What would you do there?" I asked him.

"Write."

BOB AND I HAD TALKED in the coffee shop for about thirty minutes. He didn't bring up the incident where I repeatedly sent him text messages from O'Reilly's, asking him to eat a sliver of peanut butter cup with me one day.

Afterward, we went outside the coffee shop and we both had a cigarette. He had two left to be rationed for the evening.

That night was cold, there was a bit of ice on the ground and sparse, drifty flakes swirled into the centre of the road.

"I see you all the time with Johanna. You know, she's right there." Bob said.

"She's working. Why didn't *you* talk to her?"

He didn't really say, but he suggested that he doesn't really talk to Johanna very much.

"She's okay. I'm kind of seeing someone else and it looks bad. Plus I don't really have anyone to talk to about it."

"Why don't you talk to her then? What's going on with you and her?"

"Johanna has no job and when she's in town she's holed up at some guy's house. I don't know what he does but there has been some suggestion from her friends that I stay away for my own safety. I really don't know what's going on there, but I haven't seen you in a while."

"Does it bother you that she has no job?"

"No, not really. Just that it costs me a fortune to see her. It costs me a lot of money to have to buy her beer every time I see her. She invited me over a few times, but it usually results in her texting someone else to find somewhere to go and then I go home. I've invited her over but she doesn't want to come. I have my problems too buddy."

"Ya, I could tell."

"I lost my job at the coffee shop. And I lost my job at the marketing place."

He didn't respond.

I had bought pink cancer awareness tic-tacs the day I met with Eileen for our first date, and it was the fibromyalgia she suffered as a result of her cancer treatment that made our sex so difficult. I felt nostalgic about Eileen still, not anywhere near in love with Nadine or Johanna, but not nearly as suicidal as I felt in the winter when Bob made that sincere gesture to console me and listen to music with me, better than when I started seeing the therapist at the university.

At the end of my first year of university, I was seeing a psychotherapist at the college. One of my professors drove me to her office when she noticed I was being followed, harassed, and bullied by a young female undergrad. The therapist was a tall, gorgeous woman who I had seen before, buried in a memory somewhere. She looked like a lawyer that I had an involvement with a long time ago.

"Do you do any drugs," she asked.

Therapists always seem to ask this question, almost like it's some sort of deal-breaking thing, when completely contrary to the stigma attached to the drug trade, the most stabilizing factor in the medical profession, at least at a financial level, seems to be the pharmaceutical industry. It comes off as a question more like, are you a cop?

So I say something simple, like, *I like to unwind with a tiny, tiny little morsel of—*

And I could see the anticipation in her eyes. I had hardly looked at her to respond, and I could see and feel the anticipation in her eyes.

Just to be clear here, the problem at the university and work has to do with little teenage girls who can't last five minutes without orgasming all over the donuts and metal corners of coffee machines when I'm at work, and barbells at the gym, and metal encasings in the halls that house firehoses.

There's no place for the women to go. Not in their shared living quarters with paper-thin walls, or in the bathrooms with hard and cutthroat women and fire walled internet connections, and I would have no problem servicing them at another place at another time, but they simply don't know what they're doing. I'd get her to the door, see she wants to come in, and I'll invite her, undoubtedly I'd invite her, but she won't come in.

Every now and then, I'll be in a Wal-Mart or thrift shop, and some lady will look at me, walk into a corner somewhere and stand there with her backside facing out and look back at me like, what are you waiting for?

"I smoke a little pot with a guy in my building complex. It's rough because he knows what I'm going through. But they're all young guys," I told the therapist.

"Where do you get it?"

"I know it's not legal, but it's going to be legal soon anyway, and I just get it online. I don't need much. A tiny amount lasts me months and months. Plus, I don't feel so depressed when I smoke it. Not like when I drink alcohol. I don't think it's that bad. I mean, the doctors, if I tell them I'm suicidal, they'll give me enough pills to kill me anyway. I'm trying to do my best to get off the death wish medication the doctors are giving me. Really, pot's not so bad. At least it makes me laugh. I mean, what do you think? Is it bad?"

"You aren't obligated to take any medications."

"That's what I told them. But lets say I get really depressed and suicidal, there's no support for me. I go to the hospital and if I don't take the medication, they get a team of security guards forcing me to take pills. The psych ward at the hospital is not the same for men as it is for women. Women can come and go. The doctor says to me before the last time I went there, 'The nurses will talk to you.' I was in there for three days and none of the nurses will talk. Actually, they literally tell you to shut up and take a pill or else the security guards will force me to."

She didn't say anything. She looked at me sort of insisting I go on, to continue talking to her. So I did, for months, throughout the spring and summer, until I left the university for art and marketing work.

Before Bob left the coffee shop to have a cigarette with me, I asked him to read a short story I had sent to a magazine earlier in the month. I thought if one of my short stories was published it might impress Eileen, somehow making up for getting canned from the marketing company.

There had been a West Coast magazine that had taken some sort of initial interest in my writing work in a way that, afterward, seemed mostly to humour me and pilfer any kind of enthusiasm I had for their publication to subscribe to it. I was enthused—for a while—so I paid for a subscription, but I've since called them almost a dozen times to let them know I still haven't received a single copy.

I handed him my phone. He began to read the story:

I Mugged John Lennon

Johanna had no job and when she's in town she spends weeks holed up at her coke dealer's apartment. I say that in a non-judgmental way. I'm no better, I have a record. But, there's no Wi-Fi at her dealer's apartment and Johanna can't afford a cell phone contract. Before she went away this time, we often spoke on the phone late at night, the only time she could sneak away to the outside of the

Pizza Hut after hours to use the Wi-Fi.

She leaves for months to go to her mother's apartment up north to sweep the dust. She's been away since the beginning of July and I hope she's back in time for my book release. I'm hardly able to request that she promise to be at the book release with me at the beginning of August.

The text message conversation I had with my manager just after 9 AM this morning went like this:

Manager: Yo, what's up?

Me: Hey. Was I supposed to work today?

Manager: Nope. You probably know what's up. I was going to tell you to bring in your uniform tomorrow when you pick up your paycheque.

Me: What paycheque?

Manager: Beats me. Did you not work at all in the last week, or the week before?

Me: Nope.

Manager: Ah, okay. Either way I need your uniform.

Me: I've already got an offer for it on Ebay.

Manager: Seriously?

Me: Haha. Ya. $15.

Manager: That's it? Did Andrew suggest you do that?

Me: Are you trying to get rid of him?

Manager: No, wasn't planning on it. Why do you ask?

Me: Just wondering if you wanted me to incriminate him.

Manager: You already did.

Me: No I didn't.

Manager: I just need the uniform.

Me: You can come pick it up.

Manager: I guess I could, but I don't even know your living situation anymore.

Me: Do I have any shifts this week? I forgot to ask.

Manager: No.

Me: Ok.

Manager: I was trying to be decent and talk to you in person. It's not working out with you. I was going to talk to you in person when you brought in your uniform and got your paycheque, but with no paycheque and beating around the bush, didn't look like that was possible.

Me: I don't want to work there, dude. I don't care. But you're going to have to pay me for my time to bring in the uniform.

Manager: Pay you for what time?

Me: Otherwise, you can come pick it up and I'll take it out of my jar of turpentine for you when you get here.

Manager: You want $3?

Me: $120

Manager: For what? I wanna know where you got this number.

Me: Two hours times my rate of $60 per hour. Time is money.

Manager: Not that much.

Me: Then I won't do the job. Call a messenger service and have them pick it up, and I'll take it out of my jar of turpentine when they get here.

Manager: You do love the word turpentine. I'm trying to be decent and you choose to be difficult.

Me: Thanks man, it's been swell.

Manager: Okay, I'll go pick it up tomorrow since it isn't worth your time.

Me: Alright. My address is 1499 N Chestnut St., Wahoo, Nebraska. I can't promise I'll be there on time. You know us Wahoos.

Manager: Okay. See you at 7.

Me: Are you done work at 7?

Manager: Yes.

Me: I have a meeting tomorrow. I don't know what time yet. I'll get back to you tomorrow, or the next day, or the day after that, or after that. Certainly at some point.

Manager: Yeah, when you give someone a fake address, you don't give them the state name, or the fact that you won't be on time, even though you didn't specify a time.

Me: How is that a fake address?

Manager: Well, sorry, not a fake address, an address that is not yours.

Me: I'll be there drowning my tears.

Manager: You can't drown tears.

Me: It's a personification. I'm a bit of a poet. I'll give it to Andrew.

Today I took out a high interest loan for $2000. I immediately bought a longboard, copies of my book for the release, a slice of pizza and four pints of Budweiser. I shouldn't have had to buy a new longboard but I have been lonesome while Johanna is up north, consequently sitting near the liquor store for a while, waiting for at least one of five people to respond to the messages I sent them asking if they wanted to eat a quarter of a peanut butter cup with me.

Some woman sidled over and asked me to buy her alcohol. Apparently she had been banned from entering the liquor store, so I took her ten dollars and brought back her order, then she asked if I wanted to drink with her. We went into a nearby alley and I noticed a police car drive by as she repeatedly asked to use my phone. Her requests became increasingly more dire—it right creeped me. I chugged down the rest of my beer and ran away from her. The worst part was, I left my longboard with her as I bolted.

I was shortlisted for the first time today. It seems to be a bit of a lucky streak because Johanna returned yesterday. She used the Wi-Fi on the Greyhound to exchange texts with me for the entire two-and-a-half hour trip and we started drinking in her living room and backyard when she got back into town at two in the afternoon. We must have made three trips to the beer store to replenish the supply of beer before 7PM rolled around. We planned to go to the rock show at the bar. I was able to afford a couple beers at the show or get a handsomer batch to leave in her fridge for later.

She spent the entire time at the bar texting her dealer. He was being possessive and was upset because she chose to see me as soon as she got back into town.

We opted to watch the show dry, and after the show we came back for the tall boys I had left behind, but there were about six red roses ominously waiting for her on the doorstep. She wanted to leave her house because some of the messages from her dealer had been threatening and she didn't want to be in any danger while she was disobeying him. We made off to the lake with the remaining beer.

Sitting on the top of a picnic table admiring the lake, I started gesticulating animatedly as I spoke so that it wasn't obvious I was inching closer to kiss her and she asked me to lie down on the picnic table to join her in appreciation for the stars. July was hot, the beginning of August cooled off a little, and as we gazed into the darkened, speckled sky I told her I had to hit the can. I didn't know where to go so I took a leak right in the middle of the park, facing the main drag and the lights of the city. When I turned around, Johanna was about to be splashed. She was facing the lake, sitting on the picnic table, having a drink of beer. She was dimly lit by the lights above the path around the bank of the lake.

"Oh! You're gonna get it!" I said.

"What?"

"The sprinklers are about to hit you … right now!"

"Come here, this feels amazing!" she said.

"No," I walked closer.

"I want to get totally wet!"

"Why don't we jump in the lake?"

"Okay!" She started toward the beachy area.

"Are you serious?" I followed her.

She pulled off her sweater and I took off my shirt. She unbuttoned her white blouse. We got to the beach and she undid her skirt at the back. I was enamored by how she looked in her pink panties and matching bra. She walked into the water as I pulled off my tight skinny jeans. It worried me that the water would be chilly because the temperature was unusually cool for early August. "It's nice," she said.

"Thank God." I got in.

I had no idea what time it was, no one was around,

our last two half-drank beers sat atop the picnic table and the most beautiful woman in my life was floating in the shallow water as I skipped rocks around us. She came back in closer and I knelt down beside her. It was silent and sweet serenity came over the beach. She began talking about the stars like they were her best friend, but it came off like a drunk trying to make a friend at a bar. "I love you, stars. You're my favourite stars ever." I laughed. She stopped carousing with the stars and it was silent once more.

Too romantic, I thought. Our bodies made faint swishing and gulping sounds as we hushed, torso-immersed at wade-depth under starlight. "This is so romantic," she said. I sharply leaned in to kiss her and it was pleasing that I was able to touch her entire body as she floated.

"What do you want to do?" she said.

"I want to, but I didn't want it to be this wet."

She laughed. We got out of the water and I looked at my phone. "It's 1:59," I said. We had been drinking for twelve hours.

Johanna has been mostly unreachable since the day she came back from up north. We had a video call early this morning as she huddled near the awning lights of the Pizza Hut entrance. A strange conversation. When she wasn't speaking, her mouth chattered conspicuously, unaware that her entire face expressed an emotionless void. Later in the day she didn't respond to my messages asking to see her.

I've never talked to Johanna's roommate before but she asked me to meet her for coffee this morning. We met at one of the coffee shops downtown before most of the businesses were open and other than Kira and I, the patrons were all sullen men, with languidly drooped heads over their tables. It wasn't obvious enough to say that she had asked me to meet because she was worried about Johanna, but an air of warning loomed over most of our conversation.

She does drugs there. He's a dangerous guy, you should be careful. His ex-wife was unable to convict him of assault. She says he's a changed man but she never seems okay anymore.

I've had considerations about Kira's words all day.

Johanna finally spoke with me tonight. She says she's okay (she even had twelve dollars) but I've been worried and don't want to anger her with accusations of the dangerous man she stays with. She asked me to meet her at the bar for a beer and despite the university orientation today, and first day of classes tomorrow, I'm headed out to meet Johanna anyway.

"I don't think twelve dollars is enough for two pints," I said.

"Is it enough for two bottles?"

"I don't think so."

"What are we going to do?" she asked. I thought for a second.

"I remember when I was about six years old, this old guy in the neighbourhood used to walk by on his way to the legion. He drank everyday at the legion. My sister and I, and a few other kids, noticed when he walked by, some of our toys and stuff would be missing—like, it was a small town, so things like that were unusual. Everyone called him Boo-Boo."

"Why did you call him Boo-Boo?" she asked.

"I don't know, but we asked him why one time after he just left the legion. He said, 'want to see my boo-boo?'"

"Want to see my boo-boo? What did he do?"

"He lifted up his shirt and he had an enormous outie belly button, and a bunch of us kids were like, 'Whoa! Gross!' He asked us if we wanted to touch his boo-boo."

"Oh my God!"

"Yeah, so one day, he's walking by, and my sister and I wanted some candy, so we decided to rob the old guy. It was pretty bad, but we were kids, and he was always stealing our stuff and being a creep. So, we went up to him and held him there, looted his pockets, his money, wallet, keys, everything."

"What?"

"Seriously! We looked at his ID. You know what his name was?"

"What?"

"John Lemon," I said in the noisy bar.

"John Lennon?"

"No, John Lemon."

"So, what happened?"

"We were good kids. I still am, really. I showed my dad because

I felt guilty. I was like 'Dad, I got this guy's Driver's License.' He was like, 'Who?' I kind of mumbled my response, 'John Lemon.' My dad looked pretty excited.

"My dad said, 'You got John Lennon's ID? Lemme see that,'" Johanna laughed at the story.

"Did anything happen?"

"We got our candy."

"Okay, so what should we do?"

I weighed the consequences for few seconds, then looked convincingly into her eyes.

"You wanna rob an old man?"

"Come on!" she said, grabbed my hand and we dashed out of the bar and down the street.

"Wait here."

She walked up to a middle aged, fat, bald man on the corner of the strip talking to a young blonde woman.

I don't know what was more pathetic: that moment, or missing my book release party. I avoided staring to disguise my intent. After a minute or so, Johanna pointed at me. The young blonde walked out towards me. "You! You mugged John Lennon! We want you! You coming?"

"Where we going?" I asked.

"We're having a party. Wanna come? I wanna know all about the man who mugged John Lennon!"

"I'm invited?"

The bald man hailed a cab and it wasn't long before we were at his apartment. He had no table or dishes in the kitchen, or furniture other than queen sized mattresses in the bedrooms. The living room had a television, a coffee table, and behind one of the couches was a fully stocked rack of alcohol with opened bottles of Blue Curaçao and Sourpuss.

"Do you like Porn Stars?" Danielle, the young, attractive blonde asked.

"Never had one."

"Cheers! To the man who mugged John Lennon," she said, and then everyone yelled, "Aye!"

Danielle had a shot already poured for me as soon as I had the slightest notion that I might like another. The shots kept coming, one after another for all four of us, but every time she gave me one, she said, "To the man who mugged John Lennon," and everyone yelled, "Aye!"

Bill, the bald man kept mentioning a magazine he had started several years ago that made him a lot of money selling it off, but didn't move a bit the whole time we were there. Danielle sat on his lap a few times, flirting with him as much as she flirted with Johanna and me. I was blathering nonstop, in a voice punchy enough to penetrate the loud punk-rock music. "Another shot?" I heard Danielle ask me. "Of course!" I said.

She appeared to me with the drink, bare-breasted, at the side of the couch. She walked over to Johanna, handed her a drink and started feeling Johanna's breasts. The two of them started making out. They walked over to the tableless kitchen, that, for apparently just this reason, had a stripper pole. Nobody spoke for a few minutes, the music was loud, and when I looked at Bill, he had a huge grin on his face.

He glanced over at me and said, "I think they want you to look at them too."

I looked. The two young women were completely naked, dancing around a thick silver shaft, pointing at us men.

"I have to take a break," I said, and walked out of the first floor apartment, over to a picnic table in the yard. I sat there wondering about the situation, how I would get home in that state—and mostly—that I wanted to have a go at both of those women more than I wanted to see tomorrow.

I went back inside after a few minutes and Danielle greeted me: "I'm sorry hun, but I think Johanna is going to be staying with me tonight. I'm going to get you a cab home."

"Okay, I was just about to walk home anyway," I told her. She called a cab, and walked me outside to wait, wearing one of Bill's sweaters to cover her ass.

"Take my number," she said. I took her number, told her she was wild and sexy, and that I would talk to her soon.

"I should set an alarm now because I have to wake up at 7AM tomorrow to get to my class," I said.

"What time is it now?" I looked at my phone.

"3:53."

"There he is. That's my guy, he'll get you where you need to go." She walked up to the cab window to speak to the driver. "Sorry, it's not me tonight, babe, just a friend. I'll talk to you soon," she said to him and opened the door for me.

"Get in. Talk to you soon," she instructed.

After that, I remember waking up to go to class, sitting in the shower, drunk, rubbing my soaking face, unsure if I was crying, or alive to even do so.

I did my best, but I was still late.

"Who's next?" the professor asked immediately after I walked into the small auditorium. "Looks like we have our next contestant, right here. What's your name?"

"Brad, but people call me Ox," I said, furtively.

"Why don't you come up to the front and tell us, in two minutes, why you had the best summer ever?

fin

Bᴏʙ ғɪɴɪsʜᴇᴅ ʀᴇᴀᴅɪɴɢ ᴍʏ sᴛᴏʀʏ. "Is this true?" he asked. Johanna was still there in the window in the front.

"Mostly," I told him. Like I said, I didn't make it to any of my classes when my second year started. Other than making it to that first class of the year, the story Bob read was true.

By the time I met Stefi in the following summer, Bill, the guy in my story, had slashed his forearm from his wrist to his elbow in a place on his arm that had a tattoo that said *Never Let Them Win*. He came out of the hospital with at least a dozen stitches and lasted only another few months on the outside. He died of another suicide attempt.

I stood in front of O'Reilly's with Bob and Aiden a few weeks before showing Bob my story, on a windy, snowy morning. "What's your book about?" Aiden asked.

"It about the connection between love and music. The couple in it connects through a love of The Beatles."

"I don't like The Beatles," Bob said.

"I admit, John Lennon was kind of an asshole," I said to Bob. "Paul's songs were nicer. You know they were raging back in the late 60s. Everyone wanted a piece of them. It was amazing how Paul made love to the camera on that last performance, in that rooftop concert."

Bob didn't respond and then a man across the street, unkempt, and in raggedy clothing started a commotion. The bum was shouting and in a tiff with no one other than himself.

"What's this loony up to?" I said. "You know its funny everyone's so sycophantic."

"What?" Aiden asked.

"Sycophantic. It's people's obsession with famous people. Like if this crazy bum across the street shouts something, people yell at him to shut up, but if John Lennon said the same thing, people would be like: *I'll give you a million bucks for that.*"

Bob went back to work and I left O'Reilly's to smoke some bongs with Alex at his place. I no longer lived in Alex's building complex but I still had been seeing him there every couple of weeks for *salads.*

Alex finished his degree in the spring, and just before I met Stefi, he moved back to Brampton. He was one of the few friends who read my first book. He said he really liked it, but I was concerned that it spooked him—because he was such a young man—that my book left an impression on him that life was exceedingly bleak, that I had registered in him some lasting thoughts of my growing 30-something apathy, negativity, and futility. Even still, I sensed he felt encouraged to live well at any age as a result of the magic contained within my first book, besides whatever negative auxiliary messages may have resounded.

The comfort Alex brought me was undeniably the best part of that period of my life, as we studied art and design together—especially amid the frequent suicidal thoughts in my mind at that time in my life. At the time, I felt it couldn't be a mid-life crisis. *Early 30s is much too young an age to have a mid-life crisis*, I thought.

"The problem I have with my medication is a problem of the external world not changed because I'm on this Paliperidone. If a woman doesn't choose to be with me, it's going to be no different on or off the medication. The medication just makes me gain weight, and less desirable to women. The problem I have is that I don't want to manipulate a woman into loving me, and I want her to choose me of her own free will. No woman has ever really chosen me. It makes no difference, externally, whether I take this medication or not," I told the therapist. "I feel better when I smoke weed, at least for a little while. I'm going to try this out and see how it goes," I continued, explaining my reasoning for quitting my medication in January. "The only thing is: I can only do it in small doses at specific times, because it prevents me from thinking and doing things that require a specific focus level, like reading and writing. That's what worries me. But it makes me feel better for a little while, like an escape from reality."

Alex brought me into a world of his steadfast love for cannabis. The cannabis highs he loved were well-suited to the psychedelic art he appreciated and modeled, much to my own wonder and appreciation of him and his work.

The night I moved into my house near his, we searched a party that was happening in the common area of the apartment complex for a half-o to replenish what Alex had to smoke. We never found any that night, but he had a shipment coming from BC in a couple of days.

"Do you want to have a salad?" I'd text Alex after classes, when he still lived in my building complex.

"I can do that. I'll text you when I'm good."

An hour or so later, he'd have me over, "I'm good now," he would write.

"Here," I would write to him, standing at his door.

We listened to Mac DeMarco's *Salad Days,* and other mellow stoner rock, while inhaling the smoke of *the salad* through his newly cleaned bong. Alex was very particular about keeping his bong clean.

The night that I was supposed to start touring with Nerds, I found myself in a nexus of Brampton lost and found. It was purely by accident that I had ended up somewhere in Brampton that April afternoon.

I stepped on the bus that I thought would have me taken to the Nerds tourbus, and I sat on my seat, reading William Carlos

Williams, hardly putting my head up, about ready to take the open road with the band.

The funny thing is, I wasn't on the wrong bus. I looked at the bus sign after I got off, after going through Etobicoke, Mississauga, and finally Brampton, and it was the right bus, but it just took a detour, so far away from where I was required to be as a timely roadie.

I looked up, and a cute brown-skinned woman made her way directly to my seat. Then a few stops later dozens of brown-skinned people started getting on the bus at every stop, until the bus was full of people. The cute brown-skinned woman sitting beside me had sat right on my bookmark. Coming to the realization that the bus wasn't headed to where I was supposed to go, I had the thought to ask for the bookmark so I could get off the bus to reroute, but I didn't feel like disturbing her.

She turned to me and said, "It's nice tonight, isn't it?" I looked outside and a misty snow fell in the lingering and waxing daylight, spring warmth anew.

"Yes, it is. What's your name?"

"My name is Nav," she said and held out her hand.

We shook hands and she got off the bus two stops later. I hardly had time to ask her anything more.

I thought of visiting Alex, but I didn't know where he lived in Brampton, so I put my head back in my book of William Carlos Williams poetry, focusing little on where the bus was taking me, on its excursion from the norm, from reality.

Further into the dream, I thought that because Williams was a pediatrician he would have to be very clean, and I might invoke some therapy about the childhood enjoyment I wished that I could, in some ways, have back. And I felt my eyes were seeing the cleanest thing they'd ever seen in a book, seen anywhere, and I felt taken, like a mantra—white, fluffy snow falling so pristine, in slow motion—falling into the dream, grasped in the snow's rubato rhythm, taken somewhere clean and good, and necessary.

I was reminded of how clean Alex was, with his lackadaisically parted blond hair, and neat fashions, and clean psychedelic artwork. The bus had found me in the essence of what about Alex that saved me from hailing all the memories of loss of love that had plagued my consequently suicidal mind a year prior. Everything was clean, and everything had to be cleaner than before, moving forward. I was cleaner missing the tourbus, I knew then.

I looked up after it had been some time passing, cracked my neck, side to side, forward and backward, and we were near the underground entrance to King station. I took the subway from Union, up to Bloor street and back down the Bloor line into Bloor West, home.

Various
Positions

Various Positions

Guerin. Guerin Tracy. The singer in Nerds. I had arranged to meet with him at O'Reilly's at the end of December before I knew about Megan's New Year's party. We had arranged to meet for nine o'clock but I went to the bar a little early to have a drink and lubricate. Guerin was there already, with a pretty blonde singer who works at one of the fancy cheese shops in Kensington Market. I sat with them wondering when I'd start my interview with Guerin. We kept drinking.

Bob finished his cooking shift later on and came to drink with us. He bought me a pint when I ran out of money for beer. Eventually, Guerin, Bob, Aiden and I left the pretty blonde alone at the table as Guerin and I went with Guerin to do our interview in the private bathroom in the back of the bar. I sat on the sink, and Guerin looked like a drunken, drugged-out rockstar sitting on the toilet.

As I asked him questions, it became clear that we were both too drunk to do the interview. I had a contract with Martin's magazine to get this interview on a recording and transcribed into a written document within a few weeks.

I knew he loved the book *Brothers Karamazov*, so I asked him a question about it. He didn't know what to say, almost liked he'd never actually read it. "I know there's one person in that book I'll never be like," he said, then trailed off repeating the words, "I'll never be like that. I'll never be like that."

The response was like a street pedlar being interrogated for information by a cop on the street. I supposed I looked like a cop because I was wearing a suit. I wanted to look professional, but Guerin seemed to have other ideas. I think he became insecure that his wits failed him as I asked the intellectual questions I had prepared, and his lack of accustomed rehearsal time in performing for my voice recorder made his answers seem boring. I felt tired of his simple answers and a feeling that we were going through the motions on what would turn out to be an incredibly boring interview for the magazine was in the works. A feeling Guerin seemed to share as well.

Aiden came in the bathroom. "What are you guys doing in here?" he asked. He probably thought we were doing lines. As Little Hollywood once told me: "Guerin's been doing coke since I was seventeen."

"We're almost finished," I said.

"You gotta get out of here," Aiden warned.

I guess the interview turned on me when I asked about Guerin's trademark Kikkoman Soy Sauce shirt. Supposedly, the semi-famous singer was a little insecure that he had gained some weight and his trademark shirt didn't fit him anymore. Front men in bands, I've noticed, are often quite sensitive about appearances. But, I couldn't turn the interview around after that.

Despite the failed interview with Guerin Tracy in December, as I walked into O'Reilly's on New Year's, I ran into Martin French on the busy strip. Thousands of people undoubtedly drunk, stoned, passing by. Shell was at his side.

"How's the new job?" Martin asked.

"I lost my job at the Marketing company."

"You'll write for Smash."

Smash was a popular music magazine that he had started when he still worked as a door man. I was happy that he made the offer, and it had always been a bit of a goal of mine to get some pieces in *Smash* at some point. Martin didn't have to know that my last interview was a total bust. Embarrassing to say the least.

"Don't go to O'Reilly's now," he said.

"Why, what happened?"

"Shit went down."

"What, was there a fight?"

"They're cleaning it up," Martin said. He said the owner was extremely pissed off about the turn out for New Year's.

Martin and Shell ran off together, like they were part of some independent movie about serendipitous, interconnected couples on New Year's. Shell always looks and dresses like a movie star when she goes out to the clubs on the strip.

I ran off with Aiden and Bob after the Guerin Tracy interview. I was remembering what I said to Liz, the pretty blonde after Guerin left us for a date he had planned. I told Liz that the interview with Guerin didn't go so well, that I wished I had interviewed her.

"I don't think it would have went as badly if I was interviewing you," I said to her. I didn't know where Aiden and Bob were.

"I don't really play music anymore," she said.

"Well, when you were playing, I really wanted to. You know, it's difficult approaching a female artist for an interview. It's like asking her on a date, when really the intentions are just for the interview. Have you read A Visit From the Goon Squad?"

"No, but I will," she said.

"Well, one of the guys in it interviews an actress, and he gets overwhelmed with lust in the interview so he tries to rape her," I said. It was an awkward thing to say and Liz didn't respond.

"I would never do anything like that, but the fact that this was such a popular book about music biz, it didn't really do me much service when trying to interview female artists. You know, that kinda thing is not my game."

Aiden and Bob played chess as we passed around a pipe taking hits of Aiden's green.

"You know I could be really close to her, I think, but I'd never really want to," I said. "She's too beautiful, and she'd break me so hard."

"Liz?" Bob said.

"Yeah."

"She's such a sweet girl. She's the sweetest. You know she has a boyfriend."

I knew this. What they didn't realize is that I had known her since she was in her first band, probably before Aiden knew her. Bob had known her for a long time.

She came outside for a cigarette after her last set one night, a few of us standing around before last call. Everyone was talking to one another and I stood there silent with Liz, the only other person not already in conversation.

"All in a day's work, eh?" I said to her.

"Yeah," she said, her voice cracking a little, like she couldn't believe I actually talked to her.

"You know that would make a good song title. You have my permission to use it sometime. All in a day's work. You know, I have this idea of everything you do fit into one day, like some alternate measurement of time. Like, what would you fit in your day, what would make your day, if you had to fit everything you've lived in one day."

"I like all in a day better."

"You know, I agree. It's not really work. You should love what you do."

"I really do," she concluded.

Aiden played the videos of Wes' anime voice over, and his clips of Wes' audition drama tapes. Wes is certainly a character.

"You know, I think I may have influenced one of the songs on her album a couple years ago," I told Bob.

He didn't care.

It was the conversation with Liz after her set at the bar, in those early days of her career. She used the *All In A Day* title and concept for a song on one of her albums a couple of years ago. The first time we had talked, almost ten years ago, influenced her album almost a decade later.

Everyone grew up since those days. I knew she had a boyfriend. Heck, I once interviewed the singer in her boyfriend's band.

Everyone knew each other, and the fact of the matter was, everyone influenced each other too. A lot of my ideas, sitting in O'Reilly's talking to Nerds during the afternoon lulls got eaten up by Wes, the brainchild of their band. The thing about me and Bob on this level came down to the fact that, although I used to play live music, I hadn't in the better part of a decade, and Bob and I were now on par, like rubberneckers in the scene. It's what I was becoming.

The failed attempt at the interview with Guerin was a good example of not being able to execute my duties as a writer, putting me on the level of a rubbernecker.

"You know, Wes is great. This stuff is amazing," I said to Aiden.

"Yeah, he is. Don't mention it to him though. I'm not supposed to show this to anyone."

"I won't."

"You wanna play?"

"I'm trashed. I can't focus on chess right now. I can hardly focus on chess when I'm sober. I think I'll go after this last scene."

Wes played both actors in dialogue with each other.

Even Wes used one of my ideas in a song on the Nerds' first album. I saw him one day in my neighbourhood, our neighbourhood (he lived nearby at the time), and I mentioned to him a few lines I thought would work in a song. I received an advance copy of the album before the release date, and sure enough, one of the best songs had my lines on it.

Aiden's apartment was on the strip, a few blocks towards my route home. It was the last time I wobbled home drunk from the strip.

I quit alcohol, and consequently, stopped seeing Johanna because of it. I wouldn't say I harboured a deep obsession or attachment to Johanna. It was easy to give up on our relationship. When she started seeing her boyfriend, he was in a bad location to meet up with Johanna at the bar, and their relationship kept her off the O'Reilly's scene almost entirely, anyway.

The time between the short hiatus with Johanna, and meeting Stefi in May that year was enough to get back into feeling like I could be comfortable with someone else, with Stefi.

Stefi wanted to be a writer. She was working on a novel, and wrote a lot of poetry, did PR work for artists, musicians, writers, and artist development work. She worked in an office in a nice location for us to be able to meet regularly. We went for power walks together during her afternoon breaks. She had a lax schedule and was free to come and go as she pleased, so our afternoon walks, after our first walk, turned into regular sexual trysts on her lunch breaks.

Stefi was very sexy. She had a great body, and I could hardly contain myself when she was bent over, naked, in front of me. What a great heart-shaped view, I guess from the cheap seats. I never saw her place.

Although she was married, I gave her an onyx heart on a silver chain. She once told me she loved the symbolism of black hearts.

Her poetry scared me though. I worried that I was the lover in the poetry she let me read. Her poetry was very critical of her lover, and it made me insecure, reading it. The strange contradiction of the insecurities she shared in her poetry, compared to the power she just oozed and exuded every time, every minute I saw her, is that she started off that first walk by telling me she had body dysmorphic disorder. Never once at any point being with her did I see any part of her personality that resembled such a disorder. She hid her insecurities so vaulted and covered up, like a buried treasure never to be found. Perhaps I did want to uncover her insecurities, like it was a fault to not see them to analyze and marvel about. But, I guess not finding them made me feel even more powerless, especially since we couldn't really be together in a full-on relationship because she was married. This made me insecure as well.

The only thing indicative about her and the connection to body dysmorphic disorder was her unfailing distortions of things I said to her, things I sent her in messages. She made implications that I had said things that I never really said, and eventually as the summer with her rolled on, everything I said to her became a distortion in her mind. Everything I said to her was criminal. I was consumed by her, but in her distorted view, she meant nothing to me.

She wrote poems of how I didn't love her, about every gesture that I made that pointed to the disinterest I felt about us as a couple. At least I think her poems were about me.

You know, sometimes I have the feeling that I'd like to be the subject of song lyrics, or a poem, but when the writer is clouded by distorted thoughts so much that the actual subject in her poetry doesn't reflect the person she writes about, you lose the wish to be a poem's subject anymore. Just a little, anyway. I can't complain too much though, she was no Cyndi Lauper.

I pulled out of that little heart-shape one day and she looked back at me like the emptiness I stopped giving her was so owed to her like she owned me.

Hey, she wasn't wrong. I specifically told her she owned that emptiness I gave her, the provisions her supposedly impotent husband couldn't anymore.

"Why did you do that?" she said.

"I just had a vivid image of my ex right there." She looked the same as my ex. They shared the same name too. Stephanie.

I called out my ex-girlfriend's name so many times to Stefi with the vivid image of my ex-girlfriend bent over in front of me that Stefi became just that. Another ex.

By mid-July Stefi and I broke up. We hadn't said we broke up, but in some sort of distorted view created by her interpretations of me, I suppose not being together anymore had already been clearly sorted out to Stefi. No matter what I said to her, she hated it.

Being in a time slot with her each time wore thin and became detestable to me. That seems like how things get when you're cheating with someone. It's like you're a trained monkey, on some sort of snake charmer leash and you do you're little trick when the charmer starts blowing the pan flute. True, cheating turns out that way, except, I have the brain of a man that will turn against the swaying charm of it all, the charming tune, and bite.

We sat in a bar at 5 o'clock. I was careful to keep my eyes on Stefi, and not the cute Irish waitress serving us pints.

"You know, it's 5 o'clock somewhere," I said to Stefi.

"What's that supposed to mean?"

I had quit drinking. I didn't particularly like being at a bar. A few weeks earlier, Johanna had asked me out for a coffee when I was still seeing Stefi every day. I talked to Johanna for a few minutes having a cigarette outside a coffee shop and Johanna asked if I wanted to go for a drink with her.

"I don't feel like being here," I said to Johanna. No bragging about Stefi, no attempt to catch up at all, in fact. The duration of time in which Johanna lit her cigarette, and handed the lighter back to me—about to leave her, after being with her for less time than it takes to smoke a cigarette—seemed to last eras. I could see Johanna was prolonging the time we were together, although I really wanted to leave. And that was the only time I saw Johanna in the summer.

Before that, Johanna invited me to drink with her on Steak and BJ day but I told her I quit drinking.

"I'm going out for a cigarette," I told Stefi.

I stood out there, having a cigarette, still high from Stefi's pot vapourizer we used on our walk that afternoon. Something about pot never really quite hit me right, and I always fight with myself to act normal on the stuff.

Back inside, we broke up, almost for the last time, and being single again didn't seem to lend itself to running back to Johanna. Instead, it seemed to make sense to go back up north, to where it all began as a child.

The nostalgic journey started on foot, with nothing other than a backpack packed with a few pairs of underwear, socks, and a few shirts, an extra pair of pants and my laptop.

I HAD INTENDED TO GO to a place called The Valley, just outside Sudbury. Gail Scott talks about Sudbury a lot in *Heroine*. She describes it so accurately, *Heroine* must have been at least semi-autobiographical, and had me a little teary-eyed to read, thinking of home. Or what once was. She wrote about a young female writer in the back seat of a car with a published professor, parked behind the Sudbury arena, a place where there's a bit of a famous live music venue in Sudbury (and likely the better part of Northern Ontario also). I gave guitar lessons to a septuagenarian twenty years ago, named Clare, who said he used to sing in big bands there in the 40s. This infamous live venue shall remain nameless, as Gail Scott left it (I respect her authority on the subject). But she says, "The place was full of writers because the general insecurity of the economic situation was creating sympathy among progressive intellectuals for the unemployed quarter of the population." And this is the way it was in Sudbury for artists: for musicians, writers, dancers, performers, and anyone involved in the whole circus of things—and as a musician you were always trying to appeal to the musicians who made up the bulk of the crowd. Northern Ontario arts is like a choir preaching to the choir and I don't regret moving down south, but I had a drinking debt to get sorted out in Sudbury. A debt that accumulated a year prior with Johanna.

Oh, and I can't forget to mention the French population, and more than necessary appreciation of Edith Piaf in such a place, which Gail Scott also noted in *Heroine.*

I'm not making this up: there's an actual knock-off McDonald's restaurant in Sudbury called Deluxe that has posters on the wall that read, *Sudbury is a one-arch town!* It even has a large fast-food restaurant sign that has a giant, solitary golden arch. There's three of them in town, actually, in each major end of the city. I strolled into Deluxe in the South End after walking from the university. I took it all in. It was summer, but the beaten paths were exactly as I expected them.

"I'll have a regular fries," I said to the employee

"You sure you don't want a family size?" she asked.

I looked back and there was a short, thin woman wearing blue jeans, flannel and a cowboy hat. She was with a tall, chubby brunette with long, shiny hair. The two of them seemed to be making some kind of commotion. The brunette seemed a little anxious about something.

"Okay, I'll go with the family size," I said. I was starving.

The employee took the brunette's order next and my order was up. I placed my fries on one of the tables and used the washroom before heading back out on the road. The intention was to surprise Mom and Dad, but if that wasn't possible, I'd get a tent and camp out next to a lake under the stars, out in The Valley.

I walked out of the washroom and the woman with the cowboy hat and obnoxious friend started chatting me up. I told them where I was from. It seemed like she wanted to offer me a ride. She told me her name and we exchanged numbers, but it started raining and I stopped in a Subway restaurant to finish eating my fries, and I had already forgotten her name.

"Hey, I just got home, what are you doing?" the woman asked over the phone.

"I'm eating my fries in the Subway. The nice lady said I could eat them in here. I didn't even have to buy anything. People in Sudbury are pretty nice, eh?"

"Listen, where are you staying?" she asked.

"I don't know yet. I stopped in at the motel down the street but they were over a hundred for a room and I wanted to try to find something for less."

"You can stay here," she offered. She asked how long I was staying and I told her I was making my way to The Valley. She drove back with her girlfriend to pick me up.

She lived in a little upstairs apartment close to the old drive-in theater that closed in the early 90s.

Beverly and her tall, shiny-haired, brunette girlfriend were lovers. There had been a man living in the spare room. He left them with all of his tool belts, tool boxes and work boots still occupying his old room. Beverly had a 8.5x11 picture of Edith Piaf at the focal point of her living room, and no television. Her coffee table had nothing on it but a tin with bud in it and a silver bud grinder.

"Why are you going to visit your parents?" she asked me, as I held her guitar with nothing on my mind to play. I put it down.

She drove deep at what made me tick. Something you'd expect from a grimy 50-something woman, in a relationship with a 20-something MDMA addict with anxiety, to get to the very bottom of the You that slipped your mind in Greyhound daydreams up to the north. Hardly anyone just asks why, at seemingly no particular juncture.

I lay in bed, looking out the open door of the spare room and looked at the large porcelain chicken on the top of Beverly's microwave stand.

"You know you have a huge cock in your kitchen," I said, as we chain-smoked over toast for breakfast.

"Where you headed?"

"I'm going out to The Valley."

"You know anyone out there?"

"Nobody in particular I can stay with. I know a guy I went to high school with but he's married and has kids now. I know a few other people, but no one else I'd really want to see much. I know a few women, but I doubt they'd see me."

"How you gonna get there?"

"I was gonna take the bus."

"I'll take you out there."

I waited for Beverly and her girlfriend, and then left out for a walk. They were still there when I got back.

"Ok, you're back," she said. "We'll go now then, you ready?"

When we got on the road, Beverly started in a direction I didn't expect. I asked her where we were going, and she said she was taking a different way.

"We're going to meet the sperm donor," she said.

We were almost in Manitoulin Island. Beverly stopped to get a 12-pack of beer. Her girlfriend cracked open a beer as Beverly drove. They offered me one. Soon enough, the three of us were drinking beer at one of the piers on Manitoulin Island.

"Where's the pot?" Beverly asked.

"I left it. I meant to take it but I forgot it," I said.

Beverly lead us on a mission, asking all of the tourists if they knew where she could get some pot. She drove us to a Pow Wow on the reserve and continued asking people where she could get some. The costumed dancers danced and the place was a chanting mayhem of people, eating, big white and black trucks parked everywhere on the scene. Vendors of little shops selling moccasins, jewelry, coins, activists handing out political flyers, and events marketers running around greeting everyone.

Beverly finally found a bud connection. She sat placid, sharing some chicken fingers and fries with her girlfriend.

"We're waiting for my guy," she told me. "You want some?"

The guy got in the car with Beverly. I waited with her girlfriend. She came back and we were on our way out to meet with the guy they had referred to as the sperm donor.

Beverly drove to a house out on the reserve, drinking in the car. The beers kept flowing when we arrived.

There he was: a charming looking indigenous young man with shiny, black hair down to the backs of his knees. I'd never seen hair so wild and exotic in my life. He had a youthful, almost pretty face in an androgynous way. He took us into a house with a large man and a little guy who was talking in Ojibway like a lunatic in a mental asylum. The little guy who couldn't stop talking looked exactly like Charles Manson. I felt like I was looking at Charles Manson at a conjugal visit.

"Take off your shirt," Beverly said to me.

"Leave you're shirt on," the little guy said to me.

"Have a seat," the big guy said.

The guy that looked like Charles Manson made me nervous. The big guy looked like he had been placed there as Charles Manson's prison guard. He was about 6 foot 6 and looked like he weighed about 400 pounds.

The infamous sperm donor took us into the house next door. His buddy was there holding a black Les Paul.

"You play," I asked him. He riffed a bit, loudly amplified.

He stepped on a guitar pedal and placed the Les Paul in its case. The five of us walked out into the yard, smoking cigarettes and drinking the beer Beverly had bought.

"Are we going?" Beverly asked.

I put my shirt back on and waited for them standing beside Beverly's car.

They drove the sperm donor back home. His friend didn't come with us.

"Wait here," Beverly said.

I waited in the car with the stereo up loud, for a long time as Beverly, her girlfriend, and the young, long-haired man went into his house.

Beverly and her girlfriend came back. "Go inside and tell him you're not his father," she said.

"What?"

"Go in and tell him you're not his father."

"Why would I do that?"

"Just do it."

When I told the young man I wasn't his father, he threw a beer cap at my head and ran out the door behind me. I don't think he liked me.

"I repeatedly asked Beverly when she was going home and she kept telling me that she would drop me off on the island and I could camp out there. I kept asking her to take me home.

The young man started getting angry with me and hitting me and telling me to get out of the car. Beverly stopped the car in front of a motel with two couples pulling their things from their cars to occupy their rooms for the night. I had Beverly's guitar in my hand and the young sperm donor asked me for the guitar back.

"No," I said. "I want to go home."

"I'm going to kill you? You're trash!" he said.

"I have the right to hit you with this and run," I told him. "Because you're threatening me."

He chased after me as I was screaming, "He's threatening me! Call the police! Call the police! He's threatening me!" We were running around the motel yard as the two couples made their way to their rooms, looking like they were on a honeymoon.

"Give me the guitar," Beverly said. I handed it to her. "You're trash," the sperm donor said.

"Fuck you!" I shouted at him.

He ran after me and and I turned around and flew. He caught up with me and knocked me to the ground and started wailing his fists in my face. Beverly screamed my name and ran at the sperm donor to knock him off of me. I was splattered there on the ground as the two couples stood at the trunks of their cars looking at me in silence, as Beverly and the other two drove away. "You're trash!" the sperm donor yelled.

The police officer came and I spent the night in the Manitoulin Island hospital. In the morning, the police officer came back and asked me if I wanted to press charges. He took me back to my room. I was hungry so I snuck out of the hospital as two ambulance drivers came in quickly through the door.

I didn't know my way around Manitoulin Island, but I was able to buy a shirt to replace the tattered shirt that I had on. I bought a blueberry muffin and set out on foot for Sudbury. By the end of the day, I stayed in a motel room in Espanola, only a forty-five minute drive outside of Sudbury.

There was a bar in the motel but I took the chair from my room to sit outside watching the cars drive by on the highway into Sudbury, tired from walking all day long.

When I got in town the next day, I walked around the mall looking for a phone to replace the phone that I had lost in the dark scuffle with the sperm donor. I ate a large chocolate bar in the high heat of the summer and the chocolate melted all over my hands as I sat in front of Wal-Mart, watching all of the people go in. *Why would anyone ever want to be a tourist in this place*, I thought.

I was desperately trying to get Beverly's number from the police officer that picked me up. He had given me his card. Finally, Beverly called me and told me I could pick up my things. I bought a cooler with wheels and a handle at Wal-Mart and wheeled it about two and a half kilometers to Beverly's apartment where my things were left in the garage. I was glad she didn't ask me back. She turned out to be a thug, just like the character in Gail Scott's *Heroine*.

I walked up near where the Greyhounds leave, but I had missed all the buses south. I stayed in a two-bedroom apartment for a hundred dollars a night up at the French community college. It was a gorgeous space that I found just before midnight that night, just in the nick of time to check in.

I looked up Stefi's email address and sent her an email. She called me a few minutes later. I told her where I was, that everything was terrible without her.

However, she was lost in her world.

Some women just have no empathy, and that's a sad truth about how women are compared to how they are perceived by stereotypes. I mentioned this as an ongoing topic with the therapist at the university—and a host of other myths about women based on how they're perceived because of stereotypes. I ranted and ranted.

"You ever just look at a woman and see that head of hers and know that there's a brain in there, and everything, and just think *that's not how you use that?* You know, like you hear someone playing guitar really well. Like, just so perfect and fine. And you think *that's how a guitar is played, folks. That's the way guitar is meant to be played.* Ya, I mean the same thing. Just looking at her. You have a brain in there. That's just not how ya use that, though. That's not how that's used. That's about what it feels like being your daddy, I think Like, as close as you can get, you know that? I'm your daddy, little girl. I'm your daddy, and that's the truth," I said to the therapist.

The therapist hardly said a word. I remember she told me she agreed with something I said once, in one of my venting routines, but I just kept focused on my venting that I didn't remember what she agreed to afterwards.

I took a picture of myself wearing only underwear and sent it to Stefi. I remembered the first time I took off my shirt for her. "You look like you have abs," she said.

I called up Dad just after midnight and he drove out to see me at Tim Hortons on the highway to The Valley. He handed over a three thousand dollar cheque to pay the debts. After about five minutes with me he drove home at three in the morning.

Anaïs Nin writes about Henry Miller's work in her journals: "I see so clearly the aim, the mood, the temper of his work, that I am able to cut out extraneous material, change the order of chapters. I told him my theory of skipping meaningless details, as the dream skips them, which produces not only intensity but power." This makes me think of how I've portrayed Stefi and I, in which the brunt of the power of our relationship has been intensified herein my writing. But in reality we only met briefly on most days, and perhaps the dream, if there was a dream, was the actual cityscape. Escaping to walks through the city in the times where I felt like nothing to Stefi, during a mostly mundane period that actually took up about three or four months of my life. Although she came on her lunch break my first day back from Sudbury, no part of me and my feelings for her could prevent us from breaking up, since we were only to ever really be a fling, in her view.

The summer—or what was really the antithesis of the dream—was made up of eating two dollar cookies from the Circle K, while walking to parks near Bloor West, looking at the groups of mothers and their children, mothers exhibiting the unconditional love they felt for the large, bulky, tattooed men they toted with them as approval of feminine prowess. This had been a notably recurring social grouping seen in the parks from Bloor West to Koreatown, and down towards the strip. Walking around that summer, longing for love, I had been in no condition for anything in that last month with Stefi, so—to be pithy—it should have been easy for her to love me unconditionally—like a woman would a big and muscular, perfectly tanned, tattooed hipster with three girlfriends, in the park.

I thought of the winters, by comparison to the clothing people in the city wore in the summer. Summer clothes were bright, sometimes obnoxiously so, and full of the hype that hipster, twenty-thirty-forty-something fashion boasts to really only other hipsters, despite the noticeable distance of courtesy Torontonians require between individuals, for personal space, safety, notably Canadian politeness, and the like. But, in the winter, Torontonians blatantly all wear black. This is predominantly true if you walk around in the south near Front and back up towards the fashion district near Adelaide, as far as Spadina or Bathurst and up to Queen. Again, you see the same black jackets north of Bloor and up into St. Clair and Eglington. And as spring weather approached, and those moments like first picking up a musical instrument as a beginner started feeling like the beginnings with Stefi, the colours and vibrancy and hype of the clothing of better weather became inspirational to the instrument of affection that took place for me that summer.

As weary as I was of being placed in that window for sex—only in the window and nothing else besides—our instrument broke, and I longed for something, any kind of replacement. The memories remained of the other sexy women I saw wearing things like tight pink leggings and flowing, windswept chemises exposing dewy bosoms, and the whole lot of beautiful—perfectly so—Torontonian women who I would never try to get close to without some form of metaphorical letter of introduction, at least to start.

Toronto becomes very hot early in the summer. Home-dwellers are sometimes seen out on the streets gardening in the dark hours of the morning, watering their lawns and pots. I walked the streets of Toronto for a night with just my backpack packed for the trip to Sudbury and noticed the early-morning gardeners. They looked back at me from within their little white-picket fences as I tried to figure out what in particular they were doing in my gazes. I would have said something, but Toronto in the dark morning hours is a sleepy little town that would hate my waking them up with small talk. Oh, the importance of everything on the home front! And in that silent space between being social and not, a space of choked desire to inquire, I felt a distinguishing separation from myself and the home front in which I pined to be welcomed.

Everything began to look like isolation to me. Millions of people around me, ready for that chance meeting, ready for the magic to start up something new, and all I saw was my loneliness and isolation. Everyone was distant to me, existing in a time and space where I questioned my own belonging. Everytime I went out to admire the AGO, or check out an afternoon set at The Rex in the dwindling daytime heat of late August, or admire the architecture of the modern addition to the ROM, or hit up a pop up pub, the reality that anyone I knew would ever find me was nil. Does anyone ever really know me? If Anaïs knew me, she'd profile me as accurate as she did Henry Miller, but where is my sweet flower, Anaïs?

As much as Stefi was the intensity fueling the dream, it really was no dream, and I had no strength to carry on until I met Franny—Francine—Franny, who was at first glance a blonde, Dutch-Canadian dreamboat. In my eyes.

Such is the way with life though: one never really knows ones destiny until it is a reality. If it were the reality of my life to meet such an attractive woman as Franny, I would never have spent my late summer and autumn brooding like a spoiled child. For some reason my poverty was not a disastrous worry to me. Hardly ever have I worried too much about money.

I was. I had no responsibility, no speakable ambitious endevours enveloping my life. I no longer talked to Johanna, Bob, Aiden. My life revolved around staring at women's long slender legs, hungry, like drumsticks in a bucket of chicken that was given to me for coin-collecting on the streets I pounded, and hounded down, day after day, looking at passers-by after passers-by, wasting away in the waning sunshine of late summer Toronto.

But I left. I had had enough loneliness. The plane of thought I was on was ugly, and that plane took me to London. On the positive, I had no debts keeping me. That plane was more difficult to leave than Toronto.

I found my way to London by train, carrying a large duffel bag with my things. The last stretch of my way was by Greyhound bus from Cambridge. I arrived in London and had an appointment for an apartment set up that night. It was to be rented by the first day of September, so I knew I had to find somewhere to stay until then. By midnight, I found myself in a fifth floor room at the Holiday Inn.

Everywhere I went, people working in London seemed more intelligent than the Torontonians I had been accustomed to meeting. It's almost as if the University of Western Ontario had popped out everyone into retail jobs like the woman working the cash at Little Caesars, and the waitress who served me a beer as I waited for a cab to the hotel. I had been impressed upon initial analyses of the people I met.

I knew I couldn't stay at the Holiday Inn for long at a hundred and thirty a night, I had to find a safe place outside with a lean-to or a tent. Luckily, I found an open door to the college and placed my hockey bag in a locker that cost a quarter every time I had to open it to get clothes, or socks, or food out of the bag. I slept on a chair near the nursing department on the second floor.

The search for a place to rent began, and I contacted people all over, walking all over London as I would have in Toronto. In London, there was an aim. I finally got close to securing a place to live. Rick, a landlord I met, probably mid-fifties, about my height with a slightly feminine sounding voice assured me, "We'll find you a place, don't worry," a couple of days before September.

Once enrolled at The University of Western Ontario to restart an MFA degree, I waited patiently for my student loan to be deposited. That would allow for, once again, having a home with a bed that had clean sheets, and that had power outlets nearby to charge my phone without worrying about someone grabbing it to toss it in a lost and found bin while I slept in a hallway at the college.

By October, days were made up of deciding what to do for food. If I had more than twenty dollars, it was either pizza or potato wedges. The pizza place I liked was down the street two blocks. My favourite place for wedges was about a twenty-minute bus ride to the plaza across from Starbucks where I met a woman for a date about two weeks before Halloween. She offered me a ride home that night and she took us on a dark tour around some industrial section on the outstretches of the city. It was almost as if she was debating chopping me into pieces. She never told me why she was going completely out of her way. I still gave her the opportunity to come up into my room, but she declined.

I couldn't remember how I came to be sitting in a parking lot outside a Tim Hortons and McDonald's outside the city, sitting on a curb. I came to, sitting on that curb, wondering which way was home. It was about three in the morning, in a place where there were no city busses, I don't remember how I got there, I actually had no home other than a locker at the college, and I couldn't stay there to sleep. Obviously, I would recognize the restaurant to the left of the curb where I found myself sitting. I knew the year. I knew who I was, and how much money I had if I had to call a cab for a ride. Maybe I walked there, and just kept walking, starving no doubt, until I came to that highway plaza with a Tim Hortons and a McDonald's. I walked with no knowledge of where I would end up, not a single thought about strenuousness or the physical requirements of walking. I just walked like an automaton until I had to sit like a primitive man about to pitch a fire, to rest, and I found myself existing in 2019 at the side of a Tim Hortons restaurant with no knowledge of how or why I was there. I went into the Tim Hortons—it was empty—and the floor had freshly been mopped.

I walked around the parking lot looking for a hitch or a place to rest my head. I believe even standing in that parking lot, lack of description how I got there suggested a gaping gap in my memory that baffled me. Although moments before, I did not exist to myself, I knew when I stepped onto that mopped floor, that I existed, somewhere near London, and I couldn't get in the backhoes parked in the under construction lot to sleep for the night. I called a cab, leaving me very little money leftover. The driver took me back downtown and offered to get me anything I needed if I just took his calling card. If I needed drugs, if I needed a woman, he would pick me up and get them for me.

"This is downtown London," he said as I exited at the college. Perhaps there was a grocery store muffin waiting for me if I only had a quarter to lock up my locker once I opened it again. The grocery store was across from the Catholic high school a block away. That Catholic high school had an exotic massage parlour across from the corner of its parking lot. I noticed it there every time I went to the grocery store. It was called Stephanie's. I went to the grocery store when I had more than sixty dollars, to stock up with vegetables for wraps, microwave popcorn, refried bean burritos, tortellini, bread and bananas. I made it on mostly a vegan diet, aside from the occasional pizza slices from Gino's.

I went to Stephanie's on my birthday. I supposed I wouldn't need the women the cabbie could have provided. Although being with that naked Caribbean woman on my birthday was mostly unsatisfying to the point of chaffing, I met another Caribbean woman one day standing at a bus stop on the way to the book store where I had previously found a first edition Ezra Pound. It was a Goodwill bookstore.

Alicia could hardly walk from the bus station, up over the hill to the bookstore and had to sit down. She had a significant amount of body weight, largely in the area of her large, hanging breasts. Her thick, wavy black hair was a little greasy, hanging below her shoulders. When I realized it had been difficult for her to be upright for such a long time I took her to Tim Hortons. And being with her made me hungry so I ordered a biscuit. She didn't eat anything.

In Alicia's mannerisms, I could see every major woman I've ever loved. It's almost as if she siphoned the core of me to steal sips of the women that really mattered. It was so obvious that she was channelling the women who were significant to me that I was frightened. She frightened me out the door in a panic, like I was running away from the possessed. She called for a ride and when I turned back crossing the street she was already gone, but not before she took my phone number to make other plans.

I had been on one other date. I suppose it was nearing midnight when I sat on one side of a coffee shop booth with my arms around a cute little woman who had just moved back to London from Calgary. She missed her ex-boyfriend and was living with her father around the block from the restaurant she bought her bruschetta that she carried to the café where I embraced her.

I held on to her, but in the same way as Alicia, she slipped through my grasp and although I had her number, I never saw her again. I became so drunk that night on only one beer—having no tolerance for alcohol after giving it up for over a year—that I thought I had been slipped a drug while I went to the bathroom at the restaurant.

After that date I felt a little more secure about drinking. Typically, the bar two blocks away from the place Rick rented me at the beginning of September had me in for no more than two pints. If I was excessively pining a woman, I'd be caught drinking three. I drank three beers at that pub no more than once, the night before my birthday, the night before Stephanie's.

I had been walking around London wearing New Balance sneakers with no insole for about two months and my feet were holding up. I walked a lot, walked everywhere. I walked to pick up Blarney in a little carrying cage I bought. Blarney was a Calico cat with white, black, and orange fur. "We're almost home," I assured her, as she crouched inside the cage, unaware of where I was taking her. I hardly knew her that day but I soon found out that she was very sweet, loving and friendly, and liked to be cuddled. Most nights she played her version of paddy cake with her paws on my stomach as I lay down on my click-clack Ikea bed in my room. I slept much better with a little new Blarney at my side.

Before my student loan money was deposited, I slept on a small air mattress with nothing other than my desk and a few pieces of clothing. I had had a woman with me on that air mattress with me before Alicia came over and broke my click clack Ikea bed, flipping over onto her knees.

I walked into Tim Hortons one night after going to the gym at the university.

"What do you want?" the server asked, rather rudely.

"Can I get a cheese tea biscuit toasted with butter?"

"Oh, that's all you want, is it?" she continued busting my chops.

"Ya, is there something wrong?"

"No, that's really easy. Like me."

"Okay, well, then it'll be no problem making it."

She handed me the biscuit and I sat near the front. Soon that frustrated employee was sweeping beside me.

"Everything okay?" she asked.

"Is there some kind of problem?"

"I need your number, that's all."

"Serious?"

"You don't have to."

"No. I mean, sure!" I said, as she walked back behind the counter. "How we gonna do this?"

"Here," she said, and wrote down her number with a thick-nibbed Sharpie. "Text me your number."

I called in the radio station at the university that night and told the announcer the story of the Tim Hortons server and he put the recording of our phone call on the air. It was a call-in show about what people were doing up so late at night. I couldn't stop the manic thoughts about her hitting on me, as disgruntled as she seemed.

If we had slept together on my air mattress, we probably would have popped it, even though she was tiny, under five feet and less than ninety pounds. But we kissed and I felt her entire body. I wasn't prepared to sleep with her on the single occupancy air mattress so I only had a half-erection when she reached between my legs. I guess she was angered, and stood at my door, about to leave. "You're gay!" she screamed.

I bought a guitar before the click clack Ikea bed arrived to be assembled. I played Lauro's *Suite Venezolana* and Coltrane's *Naima* that I arranged to be played with a tremolo melody line and arpeggiated harmony. Among various other pieces.

"All that?" my beautifully tall, slender female flatmate asked me, probing about Alicia's size, after we snapped the click clack out of my Ikea bed. I thought she was talking about the size of my guitar repertoire, but I found out she meant Alicia. The size of Alicia wasn't the worst part about the sex with her.

"Can I turn over now," as the tall Caribbean woman with large breasts rubbed oil on my shoulders as my visage faced down at her black lacy, stringy panties. She walked around the massage table and put her two hands stacked around my erotic *nachbarschaft* and looked like she was about to suck me. She didn't. She stroked hard, tight, and fast.

"I love you!" I shouted. "I love you! You're so beautiful! Will you be my girlfriend?"

"No."

"If I see you in public can I talk to you?"

"No."

"Okay, I won't say anything to you, but know that I still love you." Then I was turned off and chaffing. I put on my clothes and said goodbye, and walked out past a fat woman waiting in the lobby for her turn. Realizing she probably heard me shouting in the room with the Caribbean masseuse, I felt embarrassed. I remembered her from the Tim Horton's line as she eyeballed me ordering my biscuit before the massage.

"Come in! You know everything's on video. We have you on video walking around in front of the building. You sure you're in the right place?" the maitre'd said to me hours before my massage as I peeked in the door.

"I do that anyway. I walk a lot."

"Have you ever done this before?"

"No."

"Don't be shy, come in. Have you been to one of our strip clubs?"

"I've never been to a strip club."

"You should." I checked out the sign with the prices.

"Do you take debit?"

"Cash only."

"Okay, I'll be back in a bit. I need a shower anyway."

"We have showers."

"Couples, two-forty? What's that?"

"We do couples. You want the regular."

I took out sixty dollars from the ATM at the diner next-door and ate a turkey club in an anticipating hurry. A guy in a bucket hat sitting across from his wife glanced at me with a surreptitious nod and tip of his brim. Unusually chipper, I thought.

The following January, a female erotic massage parlour worker in Toronto was shot at by a teenaged boy, in the name of Incels. I felt like the sperm donor was right, and I knew it had been my worst birthday ever.

On a Clear Day was published in a magazine the following April. It was a story about an experience with a woman I met in February of 2014, when I was thirty years old, before I had ever had sex, before I had ever been romantic with a woman.

In 2014, I was still an undergraduate at the university. I had been living in Toronto for over ten years and I was becoming a writer, and indie music journalist, beginning to give up practicing music. I hadn't taught music for a number of years and I started to listen to a lot more rock music on the scene, rather than the jazz music I longed to be known for when I was in my 20s.

The advance copy of the story came in the mailbox at an old Toronto address around Christmas, while I was out on a day pass from the psych ward.

The package had already been opened when I received it, I skimmed the words of my story, and I gave Francine the copy of the magazine when I got back in the hospital. I'm sure she read it.

Because of my story, she told me she knew I was intelligent. "Intelligent men really turn me on," Francine once told me.

The story read:

On A Clear Day

At the end of February I was at the hospital to have a monthly Paliperidone injection for schizo-affective disorder. The doctor discusses with me how I'm doing and how my daily life is treating me. He asks me if I am sleeping well, or if I have taken any street drugs or alcohol. He asks me if I hear and see things that aren't there. Does he mean people I hear on the phone? Actors in movies? Our lonely existence is built on the entertainment of gladly being schizoid, carrying out nearly every relationship absent of tangibility. I've tried to invest my heart and soul into people, have never seen a return on investment, and it's deteriorating of self. Everything I say to the doctor is a façade and if I was to say how I truly felt sometimes, I could get locked up in the psych ward of the hospital. In actuality, everyone has the same problems as me, but the roughly ninety-five percent of people without schizo-spectrum disorders are generally a little more mentally steadfast for the better parts of their lifetimes.

The last time I was there, before today, I was late and the nurse that injects me called me on the phone when I was at the university library having a text message conversation with my sister. My sister was telling me about all the skills I have and the potential I have to start teaching music again. She moved me to tears, or was it an electronic device that moved me? No one was actually there. There were people in the library, but they were unapproachable, unlikely to be intertwined with my path. I didn't want to go see the nurse, or the doctor. I felt good conversing with my sister.

There was a time in my life when I was rude and unpleasant toward my sister, she was rude and unpleasant to me, and our malice toward each became rampant among us. These days, my sister says that in some dimension or realm, our entities chose to deliver the two of us, intertwined in our earthly bodies, to experience life in meaningful acquaintance. Therein lies the bond that defies the modern disconnect, which defies the schizoidia. It only takes one chapter, one line, or one gesture to feel arable in the Februaries of life. Other than my connection with her, I've always wondered if there could be someone other than her to partake with. A few years ago, in Japan, the terminology for schizophrenia changed from a term meaning mind-split-disease to a term meaning integration disorder. After receiving my diagnosis of schizo-affective, I began realizing that for my entire life the symptoms had been there and the resultant depths I fell into lead me to leaving musicianship behind, only to develop the belief that the other ninety-five percent suddenly became schizoid.

I said to the nurse that I couldn't go to the hospital that day. She seemed upset, and now, a month later, I look back on it and accept that she was right to be upset with me. Degeneration of personality is common among schizophrenics, so disassociation from her, my most frequent point of tangible human contact, could pose as a threat to my future.

No matter, my conversation with my sister ended and I left the library. As I walked the halls of the university, I saw two paramedics with a stretcher walking through the main entrance. They were probably students but I had a vivid mental image of the times I had been locked in mental institutions being forced to take drugs for any and every problem I might have accidentally mentioned to the nurses and doctors. Believe me: you should be honest only in moderation. In fighting any onset of psychosis and the fright that I might be locked up again, I quickly made my way to the hospital, ill-equipped for the night ahead.

I had been feeling great overall. I had just met a new woman at the university and I was friends with a self-proclaimed Indian guru who sometimes entertained me while doing mundane errands. It was a Tuesday night when I was grocery shopping with my best buddy, the dishwasher, who moved here from Punjab. He described his leaving Punjab as a kind of actual escapism, rather than the kind you get watching television. So, he made a connection with me the day he arrived in Canada for freedom. As he compared prices of chicken breasts, in the back of my mind I was thinking that Valentine's Day was on Friday. Then Vishal went to check out with his groceries and I noticed a bin that had Valentine's cards for three dollars. Vishal was charming the young female cashier with his thick Punjabi accent when I chimed in to ask her for a dose of perspicacity. I asked if she thought it would be strange if I bought some Valentines and handed them out at the university on Friday. "I think that would be cute, no one does that anymore," she said. Her timely sagacity was convincing enough that I bought the cards with my last five dollars. I procrastinated writing my name on the cards until Thursday night. On Friday morning at the university café, a blonde and brunette sat at the table next to me having a conversation. I didn't have enough courage to give them the cards. I walked through the halls, almost defeated, and went outside to have a cigarette. Not much later, that same brunette was outside smoking right beside me, so I struck up a conversation, gave her the card, and she admitted she was married. I immediately asked her about the blonde lady she was with in the café. She looked put off that I asked about her friend, but I gave her a card asking if she would give it to the blonde. I gave out cards to five more la-dies and at four o'clock in the afternoon I was sitting at the library computers with Vishal. He was teasing me for my Valentine's Day antics when Alaina sent me an instant message on the computer. She looked me up on the social network and sent me a picture of the Valentine that her married friend had given her.

I found out she was a natural blonde, was twenty years old, had two dogs, five cats, a few rodents, lived in a house that her father bought her, drove a huge red pick-up truck, and her nickname was Princess. In the following week, we drank alcohol together on a video call, sent text messages back and forth every day, and spent every bit of time together between classes having coffee and cigarettes in her truck. Meeting Alaina relieved me because I rarely meet women on a romantic level, and I considered the connection to be a small miracle.

My favourite time with her was on a Thursday last month when I read her half of chapter five from Jack Kerouac's novel, *The Dharma Bums*. It's a chapter about a character named Ray Smith and all of his friends having a twenty year old blonde named Princess at their shack in California to experience yabyum, which is described in the book as a kind of sacred Buddhist orgy. I read the chapter to Alaina, including the part where Princess sits her naked body on another naked hipster's lap, the part explaining Smith's reluctance to get naked in a room full of his male peers, and continued reading up until the part where the lead character, Smith, is sitting in a tub with Princess completely naked, making plans to do yabyum every Thursday.

Until that moment, times with Alaina were rather superficial, but when I surreptitiously showed her that she resembled, almost identically, a character in a book by an author I lauded as being one of literature's greatest, I felt as though I had transcended beyond merely being with her. Karl Jaspers, an existentialist philosopher and psychologist who left psychology because it relied on medications that did not work, and the methods of practice, to him, were futile for patients, says that our primary goal as humans is to transcend in some way, and we attempt to transcend by revealing ourselves to others. He also says that we are never able to fully realize if we have transcended because, for the most part, our awareness is only of ourselves.

It was clear that I had connected with Alaina. I knew I had transcended with the reading. "Where do you find this stuff?" Alaina said. In truth, it's a mainstay at your typical public library, but I didn't want to come off as pompous, so I said, "It's my favourite book of all time. I've read it twice." Then she invited me to visit her at her house on the following Thursday night, right after I had my injection at the hospital at the end of February.

So, I arrived at the doctor's office last month, and saw the nurse and doctor. My favourite part is seeing the nurse. I'm in my early thirties and she's older than me, but she's cute and she talks to me like we're friends and it's very candid. She knows I was a musician and one time I described to her the differences between the male and female vocal chords and how their size differences affect our aural perception because males are more inclined to hear and produce lower tones, making the sounds of females more exotic to males. I thought it would be interesting to her because she's in the medical profession.

Because it was the end of the day and my mind was fixated on the idea of spending the night with Alaina, I couldn't focus on anything the nurse was saying. "Why are you acting weird?" she asked. I told her I was going to a woman's house for the first time and I was kind of nervous. I asked the nurse if she would ask me about it at my next visit. "Just be safe and don't do anything that makes you uncomfortable," she said. I got my injection and rushed over to Alaina's house on the bus, in the freezing February weather. The sky was clear and the air was tight.

I was hungry, so when I got off the bus I went into a convenience store and bought a bag of potato chips with my last two dollars. I had no gloves or hat on and as I walked that last bit of the way to Alaina's house my hands became red, slightly frozen, and lost all agility of my fingers as I ate the chips. I walked right in Alaina's door as she had instructed. She said her dogs would get too excited if I knocked on the door. She also told me to take my shoes off in the bathroom so the dogs didn't eat them or hide them somewhere. As soon as we relaxed on the couch she offered me some potato chips.

My hands warmed up as I rubbed and petted her dogs, letting them lick my hands and face. Alaina and I lay there close together on her couch watching a movie and then some television shows, hardly speaking to one another until around eleven o'clock at night. She told me she wanted to go to bed. I asked her if I should go with her and she said no, so I told her I would leave with just enough time to catch the last bus. I didn't want to wait outside for too long and freeze.

I walked to the bus stop and waited there for a few minutes. I saw one bus pass by on the other side of the road, then my bus came and I got on. I didn't know Alaina's neighbourhood very well, had never been there before, and when I got on the bus, I realized that the first bus I saw was the one I should have taken. It was late and I wasn't sure if I'd be able to get home anymore. Eventually the bus stopped on the far reaches of the city and went out of service. I waited in the cold, direly hoping that a bus might come.

And finally one did. I flashed my bus pass at the driver and he told me it would bring me back across the city to my place. Halfway through the long loop back over to the opposite side of the city,

I fell asleep, totally knocked out and my heart sank when I noticed the bus was parked back at the station downtown and I had missed my stop. There were no more busses, and it was a blizzard.

Alaina and I didn't notice that a heavy snowfall had begun while we were together. It wasn't going to let up either, continuing to steadily crescendo as I walked the unplowed downtown streets in the biting February night without gloves or a hat. There were a few pubs open downtown and some of them had live bands inside. The pubs looked so uninviting with the large drifts of snow covering the doorways. I thought of the summer when the doors were always swinging open, and people out on the sidewalks smoking.

I became pensive of the time in my life, almost ten years ago, when I too was a coin collector, peddling pop songs for whatever compensation I could get. I felt alone on the empty streets with the snow whirling into my cold hands and face.

Yet, I became elated with a calm of surrender in realizing the magnificence of how each modular element congealed into transcendental abstraction. I immediately remembered that my disability pension for March was deposited into my bank account at the stroke of midnight that night, so I took a cab home and thought of how I would embellish to the nurse the details of a story that was only dry and exceedingly depressing in the few moments before seeing it all for the beauty of the storm.

The last time I saw the doctor, I was overly anxious about visiting Alaina, with hopes of being close to a woman for the first time in my life, to hail anything transmundane from the experience. This time, the nurse called on me and I followed her into her office. "How have you been?" she asked. I was wondering if she would ask about Alaina as I had instructed her to, at the end of my last visit.

To answer her question, I told her I had recently finished reading a book. I pulled the Kerouac book, *Big Sur*, out of my satchel and discussed it with her to seem as though I was avoiding the subject of Alaina. The nurse seemed to enjoy the musings I shared about Kerouac. His way of living and way of writing. I told her Kerouac was once on *The Steve Allen Show* claiming that all of his stories were true. "Oh yeah?" she asked sort of interestedly, "I know of that show, it was before my time though."

I told her Kerouac read an excerpt of *On the Road* while Steve Allen played some jazz on the piano. "But yeah, it's more my dad's time," I said

And finally she asked me about Alaina. She's such a curious nurse. I experienced a frenzy of excitement as I was about to recount my experience. I didn't want to let her know that my time with Alaina, sitting on the couch and watching television, was antithetical to my ideals. At the psychiatrist's office, everything in my life is perfect, any slight discourse a cause for alarm and arduous consequences, so I improvised a lacunal story involving only the seductive spirit of our closeness on the couch and how I returned home in a lovely haze, still bewildered by the magic of being with Alaina. Heck, in actuality, the story I gave the nurse was completely true, leaving out only the part about the zoological miasma. Then the nurse gave me my injection.

fin

"Hello?" I answered my cell phone.

"Hi, it's Sandra, from the medication clinic," the same curious nurse from my story replied.

"Oh, hi, how's it going?"

"Good, thanks, how are you?"

"I'm okay."

"I'm just calling because you haven't been in for your injection since January. Can I schedule you to come in for your medication?"

"2018."

"Pardon?"

"Look at the date. January … 2018."

"Oh yes, you're right," the nurse said.

"I'm in London. I'm going to school out here."

"Oh! I didn't know you were in London. When did you move to London?"

"I pretty much just left with a bag and came on the train at the end of August."

"Well, you need to take your medication. Have you been seeing a doctor in London?"

"No."

"Well, you should go to the hospital."

"Okay." I had no intention of going, and she could tell by the sound of my voice.

"Yes, because I wouldn't want anything bad to happen. I really hope you will go to the hospital."

The only bad thing I could foresee was being locked up in the psych ward for not fulfilling my duties as medical pin cushion.

"I will."

"Okay, thanks. Goodbye."

"Bye."

It wasn't the only bad thing about the situation in London, as I recalled being threatened by the security guard at my building.

"You know, people try to come in here and they really aren't supposed to be here," the security guard told me as he exhaled the smoke from his bong hit.

"What do they want to come here for if they're not supposed to be here?"

"I've been living here for ten years. Rick made me the security guard. We go way back," he said, dodging my question.

Another time, I was with that security guard, he was drunk and stoned beyond any comprehension, completely incapacitated, sitting in a fold-up camping chair in the doorway. He frequently did drug deals in the parking lot, and Rick was frequently out in the parking lot answering questions in the windows of cop cars. It was a hassle to have to talk to the security guard at the door every time I went outside for a cigarette. The day I moved in, the cigarette butt receptacle was already full, so I was depositing my cigarette butts at the side of the building as I stood away from the security guard.

"G— threatened to kill me," I sent a message to Rick, the landlord.

"Stay away from the door," he responded, a day and a half later.

The beautiful, slender flatmate's boyfriend coughed all day exhaling bong hits, which bothered me that the stench of cannabis smoke was acceptable but I had to exit every time I had a cigarette. There was a back door with an awning but there was another guy from the building standing there every night smoking blunt after blunt.

Solace, to me, as long as I stayed in the university and in London, was found working out at the gym. After having sex with Alicia it had even become difficult to enjoy what was often the highlight of my day, masturbating, alone at night in my room, looking at pictures of beautiful half-naked and sometimes fully-naked women on my cell phone.

The flatmates left me alone for over a week at Thanksgiving and I typed up a second draft of my first novelette in that time, parked in the kitchen in my underwear with my computer on a TV tray. Blarney was frequently all over my keys as I typed in front of my computer's flashy screen. I took her outside one day as a treat, and she was too timid to run away. It's good she kept close to our building because she didn't have the makings of a successful feral cat, out on her own.

"Something about California. It's like the memory is erased from my mind. I don't know what California has to do with why my cat reminded me of you," I said to Eileen over the phone, as she drove in her SUV with her daughter. "I'm just glad you answered. It's funny, I just picked up and left, and now I don't know what I'm doing in London."

"Be well," Eileen said before we hung up.

Something about Blarney reminded me of Eileen. I think I had described to her one time that my ideal cat would be a black, orange, and white Calico, and I'd call her Blarney, if I ever had a cat. Blarney had the perfect lovable, docile attitude to begin a great friendship between the two of us.

I didn't have the makings of a feral tenant in a building full of feral drug addicts. I didn't want to be there anymore. I tried to ask Stefi for a ride back to Toronto if I paid her PR fees for the day. I stood outside a nearby gas station begging and pleading for her back, as the rain poured on me, lost, a block away from the place that never could feel like home.

Stefi never called me back. It wasn't so preposterous of me to think she would drive me: at one point in the summer she offered me her PR work in exchange for sex.

I saw Stefi at a Starbucks near the Eaton Centre around Christmas when I was out from the psych ward on a weekend pass. That's how the psych ward operates. First, you make your way out of the high security seclusion area, then you get outdoor break privileges, then you get a day pass, then you get a weekend pass, then you get out. One thing leads to another, to another, and you have to promise them you'll take your medication and behave in there, and you're out. Or else you stay locked up in there. The faster you submit to their rules, the sooner you're out again.

"I can't stay long," Stefi told me. "I'm working just down the street."

She was running a little pop-up shop that had soaps and scents and candles and that sort of thing. She bought her coffee and we said goodbye. "Come into the store sometime," she said, waving at me as she walked away.

I went into her shop a few hours later. Stefi wasn't there. I bought an expensive bar of soap and told the clerk I was Stefi's friend, that it was a Christmas gift, and asked her if she would give it to Stefi for me. I left a note for her. It read: *Merry Christmas. Love, Ox.*

She sent me a message to thank me for it, but I was back in the hospital unit and I didn't get the message. Cell phones weren't allowed on the unit.

The cellphone I had been using was cracked from the fight on Manitoulin Island. The Manitoulin Island hotel owner had found it and shipped it back to me. I still had Beverly's number blocked because before I moved to London, she repetitively called me asking me to come back to Sudbury and live with her. Our phone calls resulted in her screaming at me trying to convince me that I had a lot of fun with her when we met, but I just screamed back at her that getting kidnapped and brought to Manitoulin to get beat up by the surrogate father for a lesbian family was obviously not a good time. Despite how much I disliked her—her duplicitous, conniving ways—my rent would have been much less expensive with her in Sudbury, so the idea had tempted me. Ultimately, blocking her calls was the best solution because after I told her I wouldn't move to Sudbury, she still called me asking if she could stay with me for her music business ventures in Toronto. She knew a guy that knew a guy that could make her famous. In her proposals that I should move to Sudbury or meet her in Toronto, she always attempted to convince me by offering different kinds of drugs.

I changed my number because of Alicia's repetitive calls, even after I had left university and moved back to Toronto. For days before receiving Alicia's messages, I had distinctly portentous feelings, and then Alicia would hit me with lengthy text messages about all of her anxieties. I could describe her messages as an attempt to remain as sane as possible so that she wouldn't scare me away, but still leave me concerned about her anxieties. She showed undertones of feelings of racial discrimination, but I felt that she had most likely been suffering discrimination because of her size, and the consequent lack of mobility. I had very little problem with how she looked, but when obesity diminishes a person's ability to participate in activities, it makes spending time with them less desirable, makes employment less of a reality too.

When I was back in Toronto, she persisted that I should publish the writings of her dreams. By her descriptions, she may or may not have written down any of her dreams. In actuality, her dream diary may have been another one of her dreams, which she hadn't taken the time to sit down and complete. She continued to induce portentous feelings for days before she unleashed her anxieties on me and I felt that these feelings were a dark psychic connection which she firmly held to me, that was best to limit as much as I could, to nil.

Besides, it wasn't safe to have sex with her, our relationship started out as romantically driven, and I felt she would always have that desire at the crux of her reasoning for pursuing. The reason I wouldn't have sex with her a second time is what brought me back into the psych ward again when I moved back to Toronto.

"What brings you in today," the doctor asked me. I sat on a chair in a large room where patients sat divided by curtains.

I was nervous to tell her why I was there.

"You know, I don't know if I should tell you this ..."

The doctor nodded. She looked well. I had been a wreck and it must have been plain for her to see.

"The last woman I was with Ö sexually ... she had an IUD. Sex with her was painful. I scratched my penis. She said it was her IUD. It's been painful."

"Okay, we're going to have to send you into the psychiatric unit."

"What? Why? I'm going to leave."

"No, you're going to be staying here. Stay here or the security will detain you."

I waited in the curtained off room and a tall chubby nurse came to take me to a locked room in another part of the hospital. I waited there and played with the blood pressure machine. I had no idea what any of the meters and dials did or what any of the measurement numbers meant. I thought of maybe changing careers and learning about medicine, but it would take another lifetime, and I hadn't the necessary patience to ever go through with such a drastic change. I could barely focus for more than a minute on anything.

I thought of when I was younger, a prodigy guitarist with students at a music studio, all the times I had been hospitalized in those days, and how my music was ever-so important to me and my persona. Music was the Who of me. It reminded me of the Courtney Barnett lyric, "The paramedic thinks I'm clever because I play guitar. I think she's clever because she stops people dying," from the song *Avant Gardener*, and I thought of the time, almost twenty years ago, the burned roses in my female friend's garden started to talk to me, projecting a voice from the stem, to tell me that I was an avant gardener. I broke down, bare-chested, gardening, dopamine rolling high on cannabis and Toronto summer heat, and ended up in the psych ward. I respect the intelligence of Courtney Barnett's lyricism: that song makes me feel proud to come to the same conclusion about gardening from the standpoint of a musician. But then, I thought of Hippocrates: "Before you heal someone, ask him if he's willing to give up the things that made him sick."

Was I willing to give up sex to heal? I guess as likely as the young, popular, Aussie hipster songstress, Courtney Barnett, giving up gardening because the roses, beautiful as her, take the heat to the throat in Australian summers.

"Hi," the female security guard said to me, standing next to her male partner in the door.

"Can I go?"

"No, you're going to have to stay here," the male security guard informed me.

"But, I didn't do anything. This isn't what I came in for. I had a different type of problem."

"You're going to have to take off your clothes and put these on," the female security guard with long blonde hair and blue eyes told me, holding out the hospital garb.

"But, I'm not supposed to be here. I'm here for a different reason."

"If you don't, we will have to restrain you. You don't want us to do that, do you?"

"I'm not staying here. Let me go."

"You will not be leaving. You have ten seconds."

I looked at the short, young female security guard in her padded blue uniform, and said to her, "Okay, this is for you. Cue the music."

You can't say I didn't make the best of my incarceration. I began to dance and slowly strip my clothes off, teasing the female security guard by fanning my clothes in a rhythmic striptease. I bent over, pulling off my pants, exposing my blue underwear tight against my buttocks.

"This is for you!" I looked at her blue eyes. The expression on her face was well, and unchanged.

THE LIBRARY IN THE PSYCH ward was full of junk. Mostly full of pornographic romance that perpetuates unrealistic expectations for men, full of male characters no man could ever identify with. It struck me as odd when the nurses wouldn't allow me to read the Bukowski book I had when I entered. I hadn't yet seen the collection of books in the normal patient area for I was still in the high security, segregation area. *What is this, a monastery*, I thought of asking the nurse who denied me my book. *Was it the gun on the cover?*

I found out a few weeks later that my doctor told the nurse it was okay for me to have it. The men in there get treated like criminals, the women like victims ... of men. Unless a man fits into the category of being a criminal, the psych ward will undoubtedly spring thoughts of sexism in him. My mind spun out of control, thinking of how I was being treated like a criminal. *For what? What had I really done?*

The only good part about being there, was if I stayed for a month or more, I would save in my bank account enough money to pay last month rent once I got out. I just had to let the social assistance checks ride in my bank account until I got out. Blarney was with Martin French. First, I had to get out of the maximum lockdown area with Gary.

Gary was a crystal meth addict. His body size was underweight and he had sores on his body and crusty spots on his face. Without any doubt, he smoked crack cocaine also. He would be sent into the normal patient area, and within a day he'd be back in lockdown. The first time he was sent back, he had been asking the patients around the unit for money. He pestered the young women in there. I guess another reason why those women were victims. The sad reality is that I've never really come across a woman that would be the right type for Gary, even if she was addicted to the same drugs as him. Gary held up alright, and had a sparky personality. He was quite energetic. His joie de vivre was unusual because a lot of the people I've met who became dry for a time would fall into a flatness of character. They relied heavily on the drug to be the catalyst in having a good time. To most cocaine addicts, being dry for drugs meant they acted dry also.

For me, the medication they sprung on me once I arrived in the normal patient area slowed me down, made me flat, sluggish. It made no sense to me. Drug culture in Ontario was on the rise, I had been clean, my weight was great, blood pressure great, my personality was charming. What was wrong with me was the likelihood I'd meet a woman who got sucked into drug culture herself, a woman with no education, likely had a bunch of kids, no husband, and no hope for the most part. The drugs they had me on made it more unlikely that I'd meet an intelligent, sophisticated woman, or get a job that made meeting a woman like that some kind of real possibility, especially since the injections turned me into a loafer.

My first night there, I told one of the nurses I lost a deck of cards I bought at the gift shop before being put into the hospital. "I can help you out," she told me.

A few hours later, after eating dinner from one of the hospital trays in the glassed off dining area with a television that was locked behind plexiglass, the nurse came back to me. "Here, I got you these," she said, and handed me a brand new pack of cards.

I sat in my room stacking the deck with aces, and kings. I played games with myself where I would guess which card was on the top of the deck after shuffling. More often than not, I guessed the right card. I had a knack for hand eye coordination between what my hands were doing and what would likely turn up at the top of the deck. I wouldn't call it magic, but it's close to it. In reality, we're all a little manipulative as far as ways of the world go. The little bits of magic that happen to us are often results of little manipulative ways we go about our lives. Call it serendipity, call it synchronicity, call it manifesting, but really it's intuitive manipulation.

"I feel like I'd have to manipulate a woman. No one has ever chosen me. I do my best to avoid manipulating them so they have the ability to make their own choices, but no one has ever chosen me," I told the therapist at the university. Our sessions came to an early ending, before much progress had been achieved, rather abruptly as I was leaving the university for marketing work, and one of the last things I said to her, at our last session was: "This has been great, but all I've really learned is that I think I'm going to have to manipulate someone."

I found the sessions with the therapist to be coercive. She hadn't said much to me other than, "Talk." Aside from that one instruction, she left me to mouth off to my own thoughts. There was very little inference from the therapist as to how the thoughts would progress as I vented in front of her each time we met.

"I feel like manifestation really only works if the intentions of it are good. Like you could manifest something in your life, but really it only works out for the whole of your life if what you are manifesting is good intentioned. I think that's the difference between me and other people: I wouldn't waste my time trying to manifest something if there weren't good intentions attached to it. Like, manifesting a girlfriend: wouldn't it be bad intentions if she had no control over the decisions she makes? Would it not be manipulation, to manifest a partner?

"I think this is a huge mistake women make. They see an attractive guy, know nothing about him, and make him the object of their desire and manifestations. When a man does that, it's called manipulation, and predatory behaviour. That's why, really, what works out for the best, is what's best for the individual as well as the collective of people. I feel like this is what's being decided in the collective unconscious. I could be wrong. Send in your prayers if you want something for yourself, but chances are if you're gonna get yours, you'll have to be a manipulative fuck about things," I said to the four walls, the therapist.

All of my thoughts rushed back into my mind. Hours upon hours of venting to the therapist filled my mind at all hours of the day, unless I was socializing with someone. Not being able to read my Bukowski book because of the hospital's monastery laws had been the catalyst that started my mind spinning out of control. Using my hands to shuffle, and playing a few different versions of solitaire games kept my thoughts from sending me completely out of my control.

For the longest time, to keep my thoughts at bay, I walked. I wrote books, or I socialized. Moments other than doing those things were difficult to calm my thoughts. Even walking had crept into becoming a medium activity for ruminating thoughts of borderline insanity.

In the hospital, the best way to calm your thoughts was to eat.

Gary hoarded packets of cheddar cheese in the dining room behind the chairs. He offered me cheddar cheese at strange hours of the day that often made me wonder how he had that much. Soon, I found his hoard behind the chairs one morning. And, they finally gave me a copy of *Hitchhiker's Guide to the Galaxy* which kept me away from Gary's nonsense verbalizations and ululating, and kept me reading until they moved me into the normal patient area.

"When will I be out of here?" I asked the doctor as he fanned through my Bukowski book, introducing me to my new home away from homelessness, finally arriving in the normal patient area.

"We'll see how you do," he took his head up from reading a couple pages of the Bukowski.

"You read?"

"I read."

"Not a lot of people do." I meant middle-aged men.

I looked at the trash in the library. As I said, it was mostly fodder for the sexually deprived woman. I had a copy of Jordan Peterson's book, *12 Rules for Life*. My doctor looked a little bit like Jordan Peterson. I wondered if Dr. Erickson ever wrote any books. I thought of asking him as my butt-kissing intentions began to propagate in my head, now that I found myself in with the rest of the normal patients. Gary had been out there when I arrived, but soon got sent back into lockdown a day or two later.

The first time I asked Dr. Erickson for a day pass he didn't get back to me. He met with me for five minutes on a frequency of about once a week, but was on the unit every day and I greeted him and smiled at him every time I saw him pass by in the halls. The nurse that called me in London remembered me, even though I was significantly thinner than when I had been her patient several years prior. I had been seeing a nurse who had been on maternity leave when I quit taking my injection. She was sweet and read my first book, but I only saw her once on the unit.

"You're looking good now," she told me in the summer when I was still seeing Stefi. I saw her in the hospital parking lot at the start of her shift. She obviously noted my weight loss. As her patient, she was concerned that my waist had been over 100 cm in circumference. "When you're waist in under 100 cm, you will have a better blood pressure, and the risk of heart disease is lowered."

There was a pair of women's size 16 Rockstar jeans in the hall for weeks. Nobody claimed them. I told Jennifer, the cute artist and ex-ballerina, that I wanted to try them on.

"I think they'll fit me," I told her.

"Do it."

I went into my room and slipped them on. They were a bit short in the length, but other than that, fit me perfectly like skinny jeans. They fit especially well in the hips. I'm rather high-waisted, and large-hipped. It's something I must have got from the maternal side of the family.

"You look good!" Jennifer said, rather chipper.

I was in love with her then. We stood in front of the cameras in the halls and sang Prokofiev's *Dance of the Knights* from his *Romeo and Juliet* Ballet, while Jennifer danced circles around me. I didn't know the names of the moves, but I looked at her beautiful, slender legs moving gracefully in her tight, flower print leggings. After a few weeks in the normal patient area, they allowed patients to wear normal clothes.

We talked every day. She couldn't say why she had been admitted. I didn't know if she was hiding something or she had just taken a lot of drugs and had some kind of adverse reaction. She told me she was diagnosed with borderline personality disorder.

"I don't know," she said. "It's all a blur. I don't remember."

The part she told me about her sculpture was true. One of her sculptures was on a museum circuit, and she said she received large sums of grant money for it. Her two tail ends of dogs sculpted together, with no head, called *Wag the Dog* had been placed in circulation in Canadian museums. She bragged about it incessantly. I had to bring it up several times, otherwise she would be shifty and end conversations with me shortly. It was clear she hadn't ever suffered any kind of ego-death as a result of drug use, or rejection and was still, at 29 years old, living as if her childhood hadn't yet ended, a life that childishly revolved around her, solely, and her ego. She had also been somewhat denigrating of my writing and musicianship.

"As a writer, women judge you based on how you look. If you write about sex, they don't want to read it, because they feel that only attractive men should be having sex. Most women won't read a book about a man because they really don't care about men at all other than to use them as tools or some kind of sugar daddy. Women read more, but they don't care about issues that men have. They only want to read about women. I don't know what any of the women in my book think, anything I think about them is purely speculation. How could I know? I don't want my books to be purely speculative. And because the female characters are undeveloped, women see it as one-dimensional. They don't see that it's a fully developed man, a story about a typical guy, and what he deals with. I assure you, whichever women have judged my books unfairly this way: you know very little about the people in your lives, and the only books that have all of its characters fully developed are totally phony and speculative," I ranted at the therapist.

It was all coming back to me, like another projection, for I disliked Jennifer but firmly wanted to be around her because of her young, beautifully taut and slender body, and pretty face and smile.

The issue I thought I was coming into the hospital about was never addressed by the doctors I saw in there. They must have seen some other issues that needed addressing. Most apparently that I could be available to act as a pin cushion for their medicines. But not getting rising action every day was progressive for my actual ailment because in abstinence I wasn't picking at the IUD string's scratches. But occasionally, what made it possible to do, without the pictures of half-naked and naked women I was accustomed to viewing for arousal, was thoughts of Jennifer in her tight leggings dancing and talking, laughing, and smiling with me.

I was talking to Jennifer one day when I met Francine. Francine tugged at my hand and asked me to follow her into the dining area. *A woman who really knows what she wants*, I thought.

"What brought you in here?" Francine asked me, sitting down at one of the tables.

"I had a sex problem. I'm not impotent and I didn't sexually assault anyone. I get the feeling it's been too much information for people when I mention what happened. But I'm not a criminal. I'm pretty normal, I swear. I've been in and out of this place a few times now."

"Do you know what the dark web is?"

"Yes," I paused, but quickly asserted myself on the subject. "I don't use it though. I just think it's for drug addicts, pedophiles, the criminal underground ... and people with a problem with authority. Why? Do you use it? I know people that do."

"My husband. Ex-husband. I was using my computer, then a video of me in my house appeared on the screen and it quickly turned into a blue orb on the screen then shut down after that. I found out my husband installed video cameras all over the house to spy on me. I tried getting him arrested. They said they couldn't do anything with the evidence. I took all the cameras down and destroyed them."

"How did your ex-husband install cameras in your house? You live with your ex-husband?"

"I don't live with him. It's his house. He's a multi-millionaire. He owns five houses. He never goes there."

"Well, I guess if it's his house, he can do that if he wants. What brings you in here?"

"I was with the kids and the television stopped working at Christmas. He didn't pay the bill, and he came over and he said I scratched him. I'm being charged with assault."

"Oh, well, what did you do? What happened?"

"I got flustered because of the video of me in the house and I called my ex's aunt to take the kids so I could go into the hospital. I was scared and I didn't know what was going on."

"How many kids do you have?"

"Four."

"Oh my God! How do you take care of four kids? Do you work? How do you even have a place for all of them to live?

"Stephen takes care of us. His house has six rooms. All of the kids have their own rooms. I need to fill the rooms though. I was thinking of getting some renters."

"I need a place to live. How much do you want to charge?"

"I don't need that much. How much you got?"

"I was paying six hundred at my last place."

"I don't need that much. I could do it for free if you just contribute to paying the food bills. But it's in Brampton."

"Oh, Brampton is okay. My buddy Alex lives there."

"Okay, well I don't know when I'm going to be out of here, but you just have to promise to help with the food bills and clean up after yourself."

"I can promise you. I'm really clean and I get a disability cheque like clockwork every month. It's totally consistent income.

If I'm only helping with food that's no problem. How much do you spend on food every month?"

"There's two freezers and a walk-in pantry and a fridge that's already stocked with food, so sometimes we need more food and sometimes we don't need anything at all. The kids don't live there anymore so it'll just be me and you for now, until I get some more renters. Maybe you can help me do that. I'm 44, and I didn't grow up with all the stuff people use on the internet now."

"Oh, I'm really good with that stuff. I didn't really either, I'm 37, but I studied a lot of stuff like that in university."

"Oh, you're going to be perfect," Francine said.

One of the nurses walked in and asked us to clear out of the dining room so they could prepare for dinner. Francine and I walked into the hall.

"They serve too much food in here," I told her. "I'm going to gain a lot of weight eating this much food and doing nothing all the time until I get out of here. I don't know if you smoke, but do you have break privileges?"

"There's smoke breaks? No, I just got here. Do you?"

"Ya, just since yesterday. So, you smoke then?"

"Ya."

"Do you smoke in your house?"

"We smoke in the garage."

Jennifer and another woman came to talk to us, and the conversation I was having with Francine got side tracked as the two woman started talking to Francine and I felt a little out of the conversation so I went back to my room. I thought of Francine. She had a pretty face, pretty blue eyes and blonde hair that was a little unkempt and tied back in a ponytail. Her clothes were nothing exciting, rather homely, a baggy white sweater and hospital pants. She wasn't much to think about looking the way she did but in some more exciting, stylish clothes, it was possible that she would look quite sexy.

I wasn't totally sure that she was being honest about me moving out into her house for free. The house wasn't even owned by her, and she had assault charges in the air. I wasn't sure if I could trust her.

Francine sat with me at dinner that night. "My new landlady," I said to her as she sat beside me, as all the patients made their way into the dining room to find seats. Francine and I were inseparable after that. Soon, she had break privileges and we spent the breaks together walking around the hospital parking lot and looking at the gift shop trinkets. I had no idea how she could afford some of the expensive trinkets she bought. I barely had enough money to buy a coffee on every break and occasionally Francine bought me a coffee and a donut.

There were group therapy classes during the day. Patients were asked to join the groups and participate in discussions, but it wasn't a requirement. I sat with Francine when we were both there. Some of the discussions had to do with drug use. I found out she had a previous cocaine addiction. Some of the discussions were about how to deal with psychosis, co-dependency, how to set up recovery strategies. The nurses who lead the discussions were nice, and seemed to look to me to speak a lot. One of the other guys, who seemed to digress off topic when he spoke, soon became overlooked when the patients were called on to share. I quickly found that, just like it was in high school, the leaders of the discussions preferred to hear the male patients that were more attractive, and aside from some of the younger patients in there, I was likely one of the more attractive men on the unit.

Francine always wanted to get me alone with her. Female patients weren't allowed to have male patients in their rooms but

Francine would sneak me into her room so we could talk. Nothing criminal about it, so the times when I was caught in her room they simply told us we weren't allowed to do that and I obliged to leave. I still spent time with Francine in her room when the nurses took their eyes off of us for a while.

When I was finally given a weekend pass, I found the advance copy of the magazine that published my story in my old mail box and I came back and gave it to Francine when I was back in the hospital.

"I didn't know you were a writer," she said. "Sometimes I need help editing my writing. My thoughts haven't been clear lately. Maybe you could look at my writing for my case."

"Sure," I said.

We sat together in the television lounge at nights while some of the patients watched movies. Francine held my hand underneath a blanket, sitting on the couch with me as we watched *Titanic* with the other patients. She pulled my hand, in her hand, up against her leg and when one of the nurses popped in the door to check on everyone, she let go, but as soon as the nurse left, she made for my hand again. I was slightly aroused when she did this.

Consistently, I left on weekends and stayed with Martin French on his living room futon. I hardly saw him there, and he had pill bottles all over his apartment, all kinds of band merchandise, and stacks of magazines he published and distributed out of his apartment. I wished Shell would come by, but I never saw her either. I wondered what Martin's status with Shell was, but I didn't ask.

As winter rolled on we started seeing the news of the Coronavirus situation unfolding, and at first it seemed like nothing to worry about. It seemed like something that would quickly pass in a week or two. We were stuck in the hospital so there wasn't much chance for any of us to contract the virus. A lot of the guys in the hospital were still talking about their appreciation for Kobe Bryant when he passed, that winter. The Coronavirus wasn't even in our conversations much until mid-January, when the ongoing story of the virus was brazen all over television screens at all hours of the day.

Before there were any lockdowns I was released from the hospital on a court order for six months to meet with the outpatient clinic to take my Paliperidone injections there once a month. I stayed with Martin French and took care of Blarney.

"I'm moving in soon with a woman I met in the hospital. Don't worry," I said to Martin.

"Okay, but I've been in the hospital there too. You can never trust the crazy women in there."

Francine stayed in the hospital a little longer. I was able to save for first and last rent while I was in the hospital, so if things didn't work out with Francine when she got out, I could easily get a place. In all honesty, I was just as unsure about the Brampton arrangement as Martin.

I was on a bus late at night, headed back to Martin's place, when Francine called me and invited me out to her place in Brampton. I was lucky to be on that bus otherwise I wouldn't have been able to catch the last bus to take me to Francine's that night.

I bought a bottle of ice wine, followed Francine's directions and there we were again, together, in her huge mansion. She showed me all of the rooms. Each of the six rooms had its own bathroom. I was amazed how large and beautiful her house was, that she hadn't been lying to me about it. The living room where we sat on her couch together had a fireplace and a large television with surround sound on the mantle. Francine had no idea how to use any of it, and she spent more time fidgeting with the remote than we did watching any shows. She played music videos as we drank the wine.

I had wished she sat closer to me, touching me, but she stayed on one end of the large couch, and I on the other. Our conversation was amicable, until she asked me to give her a massage. I wasn't expecting to see her that night, and I worried that I wasn't very clean and might not smell very good since I hadn't freshened up since before I left Martin's apartment during the day.

Francine handed me a bottle of rubbing oil, sat down on the floor in front of the fireplace and pulled her shirt down around her waist.

"Put the oil on your hands," she said.

I rubbed the oil on her shoulders and upper back. After a minute or two she took off her bra.

"I'm blessed," she said.

I quickly put my oily hands on her soft breasts.

"Oh God, you're beautiful," I said, softly squeezing her large cosmetically altered breasts with the oil between my fingers. I wasn't expecting to be as aroused as I was by that. She didn't really dress in a way that showed them off. "Don't you just love yourself?" I asked her.

"Do you want to take this upstairs?" she said.

"Okay, but I've been out all day. I should probably freshen up and have a shower. Can I use your shower first?"

She put her bra and shirt back on and we stood up.

"I'll show you the shower you can use. Everything you need is in there. After that you totally have the green light," she said.

"What the fuck are you doing?" Martin French asked.

"I was looking for the interview with Guerin Tracy. I haven't seen it yet. I was in London, and the whole place was under construction. Nobody had a single issue."

"London's always under construction. I don't know why I send the damn shit out there anyway. It never gets placed."

"What the fuck do you know about London?"

"What the fuck are you *doing*?" Martin asked.

"What?"

"Leave my shit alone. Sit your ass on the futon and don't go rummaging through all my shit while I'm gone."

"Where you going?"

"You better be gone when I get back."

"How long will you be gone. I don't know—"

"I'm going to Karen's for a month or two. When I'm back, you're not. Got it? You're lucky Johanna likes you so much, otherwise you wouldn't be here."

"Okay. Okay. See ya at the bar when you get back. I'll start looking for a place right away."

"And keep out of my stuff." Martin concluded, leaving the apartment.

I sat on the futon and thought of Francine, the nights with Francine. I had never felt so alive, listening to romantic songs on the surround sound, with the fireplace in the background, giving it to her like some porno movie in a huge, fancy house, after four-finger-blasting her in the hot tub in the bathroom of the master bedroom.

There was an office in the master bedroom, and a walk-in closet. There were two balconies from the top floor, and a long winding staircase down from the high second floor. We slept in separate beds for two nights there, and the room I was in had a large walk-in shower, all tiled with a seating area inside. There were walk-in closets in all six rooms. There was a balcony at the side of my queen-sized bed that had a large white awning that reminded me of something you might see at the Whitehouse. She even had an office just beside the family room with the fireplace that had been used as a room-sized junk drawer. It contained a lot of cash money, some of it American.

The kitchen had an oversized gas range with an oversize hood fan, and a walk-in pantry. The basement was locked the second day I was there, but it was full of clothes when I saw it the first night I met Francine. The basement was huge though, just a large empty space you could do just about anything with. Francine had originally suggested I move into the basement and I could occupy the entire vast area. The laundry room was next to the three-car garage. There was cash money stacked everywhere in the house. The office in the master bedroom was full of sports gambling tickets, stacks of thousands of them, as well as full of empty cans of club soda everywhere.

Like I said, it was luxurious to be there, and I hadn't felt so alive with a woman ever before. Francine even suggested we do porno movies together. She dressed frumpy, but when she was naked she certainly had the look.

"You can go to bed, then," she said, "I'm going to stay up for a while and get ready to turn myself in tomorrow." Francine was turning herself in to the police for the charges out on her.

I woke up the next day and she was gone. I worried I wouldn't see Francine again, and that she'd be in jail all weekend because she left on a Friday morning.

She called me the following Tuesday from a woman's shelter in Toronto just after Martin French left to stay with Karen. I'd never heard of Karen before, and wondered what happened to Shell.

Francine came over and we spent every day of the bitterly cold

February together at Martin's apartment. She had to be back at the shelter for curfew every night. We made love every day. Her house in Brampton became off limits because of the court case, and she rented a U-Haul to go out to Brampton to get some things, but she got nervous to go in because she'd be breaking her bail conditions, as we waited outside the house. She just rummaged through the mail for a credit card and through all of her husband's mail, putting anything that didn't belong to her back in the mailbox.

By March, Martin was staying with Karen for another month, and Francine had got an old car she had stashed away at her friend's place up north. She took me all over Ontario in that car. Mostly, she drove past her ex-husband's house telling me she worried that he was with other women. She couldn't get over losing him, which I assume was because the last of her money was in a storage locker and she was living in a woman's shelter.

She took me to her outdoor storage locker that contained nothing other than a suitcase full of twenties and fifties, twenty-thousand dollars worth of the bills. She even drove out to a field and parked at the side of a secluded dirt road to count all of the money, making sure it was all there. I suppose she had been embezzling money from her millionaire husband, who I found out owned three other houses across Canada, and one in Aspen, Colorado.

"Once you're over 20 million, you're set for life. He's worth 40," she told me. I asked her what he did to make all that money, but she never gave me a clear answer. All across Ontario she had ex-boyfriends, and she showed me where they all used to live when she dated them. I suppose she got a little annoyed that all I talked about was problems I had with ex-girlfriends in the past, that none of them really chose me. It was a permanent state of our conversations.

She complained about her exes, and so did I.

The sex with her was becoming less interesting. Even when she took me out to a hotel in Niagara Falls, we got up in the hotel room, showered, both of us, and the sex lasted only about 10 minutes, total, changing into various positions a few times. I loved the way she looked, but I don't think she was into it much, because she cut me off almost every time. I never got to finish, having sex with Francine, not once. She was too caught up in her life taking a turn for the financial worst, and I think it was a turn that she may never really come to grips about, even 10 years into the foreseeable future.

Jennifer Egan described Francine's situation perfectly in her Pulitzer prize winning, *A Visit From The Goon Squad*. Egan describes what she calls, *"Structural Dissatisfaction"* as "Returning to circumstances that once pleased you, having experienced a more thrilling or opulent way of life, and finding that you can no longer tolerate them."

"I'm done," Francine said to me. We had been in the middle of sex together.

"How could you be done? It's thirty seconds."

"You take too long."

"It's thirty seconds!"

I had been worried that our relationship was doomed, that she was dirty, a thug, secretive in a state of affairs that she hadn't ever wanted to expose about herself, what her motivations were. The stashed money, the stashed car, the millionaire ex-husband with no particular career, who was paying all of her bills, and who had stacks of sports betting tickets in his locked office, the 1500 dollars a week he supposedly paid her before her criminal charges.

When we were driving back from Niagara Falls we had made plans to move in together in her friend's vacant apartment in April.

The deal was that I would pay Francine back the money she spent on first and last month rent once I had the money to do that. I had taken up her modus operandi by not letting on that I easily had the money to split first and last month rent with her.

We went to the apartment to meet her friend, the landlord. Francine had 2000 dollars, cash in her bag. "You take it," she told me. "I don't like paying this much cash," and handed me the money.

Francine's friend had us sign a contract and I handed over the money. Come April, we still hadn't moved into the place a week after we had arranged to, and Francine already had the audacity to ask me for 1000 dollars to pay for my share immediately.

I got the feeling she blew that money with her friend on a few weeks of cocaine binging and there was going to be no place for me to live with her, even if I did pay the grand. She said her friend had already spent the money and Francine was having trouble getting it back if I didn't help pay. She could have made the sex at least a little more interesting if she and her friend were going to try to scam me out of a thousand dollar cocaine tab.

I moved back into the building where I used to live with Alex, my chum of the *Salad Days*. When I got there, I sold Blarney because she didn't like the small space, and it was near a busy street and I didn't want her to escape and get run over.

The only things I had left in my possession after moving back from London, and able to survive once again in Toronto, were a bunch of books. One of which was Kerouac's *Desolation Angels* that Johanna, as my lucky charm, helped me uncover in a bookstore. Acquiring that book was such a seemingly distant memory from where I lay my head on my new pillow. I started reading it.

I thought of how Joyce Johnson described Kerouac in her Preface to *Desolation Angels*, I thought of how Francine would describe me as she looked back on her memories of us together, I thought of how Anaïs Nin profiled Henry Miller in her journals:

"Without his writing, I don't know what Henry would be. It completes him. People know him as gentle, wonder at the writing. Yet, sometimes, I have the feeling that his gentleness is not entirely genuine. It is his way of charming. Of disarming. It allows his entry anywhere he is trusted. It is a disguise of the observant, the critical, the accusing man within. His severity is disguised. His hatreds and his rebellions. They are not apparent, or acted out. It is always a shock to others. I am aware at times, while he speaks in a mellow way to others, of that small, round photographic lens in his blue eyes. The writer is a coward. He does not fight his battles *sur place*, openly, in the presence of others."

I thought of how my own temperament, in and out of the pages, reflects Nin's thoughts about Miller. It struck me, reading the Kerouac, there and then, at that point in my life, that it seems I always go through a routine. Kerouac before—then once I've started writing the book—Henry Miller. The same pattern had been repeated when I wrote my first two books.

I see Kerouac as expanding the depth of field of what the narrative voice allows. Henry Miller because he expands philosophical planes and character sketch like a raving lunatic to the point where you think, what a raving lunatic? And you think you couldn't do much worse than Miller, which builds self-confidence. Within a sort of decanter of your thoughts, you think, what writer isn't a raving lunatic? Like a wave of self-confidence within the waves of inspiration, found between two authors, since Kerouac is like a wave, or inspiration, or medium of nothing-birth, death-life, tragic-joy of nothing's everything.

As for me: a grain of salt. All of it: with a grain of salt. In that moment. The truth found in my works is beautiful as honest artistry, as breathing liveliness, but cannot be loved as inherent truths. Especially because it was Mother's Day when I serendipitously read the section from *Desolation Angels* that read: "every evil dog in evildom understands it when he sees a man with his mother, so bless you all."

And just like that, no matter what Joyce Johnson said about Kerouac, no matter how Francine, or any of the other women thought of me, I thought of my mother, the sweetest, most tender woman of all, and I fell in love with Kerouac—his life and alikeness of mine—all over again.

Breaking Even

Breaking Even

A BAG OF TOILET PAPER, a box of cookies, bag of Doritos, and a magazine in which I had been published was left at my door when I woke up from sleeping. Johanna had left. She moved back in with her ex-boyfriend. I guess that meant he was her boyfriend again.

The last time I saw her she was in my room drinking with me, and I was raving about how bad childbirth is for women, for their vaginas.

"One kid feels the best," I told her. "Like, I'm not particularly small and with Francine and my first partner I could barely feel anything. It makes sex useless. I mean, I feel sorry for them, like, good luck finding the guy that's going to work for. They both had four kids. Neither of them even looked after their kids either. They both had to give them away because they didn't have the resources to take care of them. Francine's kids all had different last names. I looked in her wallet one day while she was going to the bathroom in Tim Hortons and I was waiting in the car, and she had all of her kids' health cards, and they all had different last names.

"Stefi, the woman that was cheating on her husband—she had one kid. She felt amazing. Even better than women who had no kids. Movies talk about how women's pelvic floor goes, and you know, it's really true. Aside from the fibromyalgia, Eileen had three kids, one she didn't even tell me about at first, and that was bad too. When we had sex the first time, I just had to stop immediately. I didn't tell her I couldn't feel anything. I've only ever been with one woman who had no kids, and that was good. She was the only woman I actually had orgasms with. That was six years ago.

"The sex with Carly was probably the best. She got really into it. She also had one kid. I swear one kid works in the vag just right. You're almost guaranteed to have two kids because the vag after one kid is so perfect. I wouldn't recommend too many kids though. It's bad for the vag."

Johanna left soon after, heading back to her ex-boyfriend's place. I guess I had scared her off, once again. It became a routine that I would bitch and complain about my ex-girlfriends with Johanna when we were living together. I can't completely call them girlfriends. They were only sex partners. The only true girlfriend I had, Stephanie, I had been in love with, still am in love with her really, and she didn't love me back the way I loved her, we didn't have sex, not once, and she married another guy about a year before Johanna moved out after Valentine's Day.

I regularly sent Johanna messages telling her that *I miss Stephanie*. Really, my relationship with Johanna is similar to my relationship with Stephanie. We drink together, and have conversations listening to music, Johanna doesn't really love me back, and if I were to have strong amorous feeling for Johanna, they would go unrequited, just like the strong feelings I had for Stephanie. This is particularly true of my feelings for Stephanie near the end of our relationship together. I had turned our conversations into bitching and complaining about all the baby mamas I wasn't having orgasms with, who made me more frustrated than satisfying myself, who never could satisfy me the way Stephanie could, if she only wished for me the way I wished for her.

When a man complains like that regularly, if she's a woman close to him, she's already on his list of past women to complain about. Some men don't do this—particularly very attractive men. The attractive men that don't are usually choked by the fact that women have symbolized them as the object that, in the objectification of him, strokes her ego, and therefore he wouldn't cough up a decent complaint. If he did complain, he would be an ego-maniac, a narcissist, in doing so.

By complaining about his relationship, he is criticizing that his partner strokes her ego by relentlessly fawning over him. The reality for less attractive men is that their closest partners require ego-stroking also, and when a woman objectifies her partner in a way that is insulting—like less attractive men usually are—it concerns him a lot less if he hurts her by being concerned with every other woman other than her, because she shows more affection towards other, more attractive men in the first place.

I notice consistently in the relationships with females that I have, that the importance of what their partner looks like is of so much importance to women that their relationships have no other degree of meaning to them other than what their partners look like. This is the case with Johanna and me, by comparison to her and her now reclaimed boyfriend.

Granted, I don't have much to offer a woman in terms of resources. A sleeper friend of mine, who I've consistently been in contact with throughout the years, who I went to high school with in Sudbury, told me around Valentine's Day that, although I smoke cigarettes, have no job, and suffer from mental illness, it is possible that I come into a relationship with a woman. But she did also offer the fact that women are conditioned to look for men with resources, particularly resources that would lead to support-ing a family.

My friend, Malek, in saying this, sent my thoughts out of con-trol because all I've seen from women is them choosing to be at the side of men with less resources and stick with them, building them up because they are more attractive. I didn't tell her this.

"I feel like shit," I texted her.

"I know you do."

I haven't actually seen her in over a decade. I met her for the first time at one of my solo jazz guitar gigs when I was eighteen years old. She asked me what the last song was that I played and I told her it was just a blues. Jazz musicians play blues too, they play it a little different, with richer harmonic variety, but since then, Malek thought I was a blues guitarist, which isn't true, and I couldn't last in most blues bands for a single set.

I've sent Malek countless letters in the mail, she bought me that copy of Jordan Peterson's *12 Rules for Life* that I read in the psych ward, and I respect her intelligence considerably. She has a master's degree and is likely the most educated woman I've been in consistent online contact with since high school. One subject that women shrug off as myth, and which they do not consider true when I mention it, no matter if they're educated as Malek, is the body standards that exist for men seeking female partners.

Carly, the one with one kid and who was amazing in bed: she told me she couldn't see me because she couldn't take seriously someone with my level of income. She went to the extent of say-ing that my income was unstable, despite that my income is more consistent than the average working person, Carly still chose to get engaged with an attractive crack addict.

Even my sister, the maliciousness that was pervasive in my relationship with my sister for the ten years that I was obese, I feel had a lot to do with my size during those years. She notably treated me much better when I was at a healthy weight. It doesn't really forgive that she was malicious to me because of my obesity.

Heck, my hairdresser in the summer talked about how skinny her boyfriend was because he was a meth addict. She couldn't believe I was single. What, being a published writer, author of two books, and a publisher makes you relationship bait, I guess. I have to admit, it was much easier to get a girlfriend when I was underweight a year ago. The expectations for men seeking female partners is a little on the disgusting side of matters. Thanks for the haircut dear, but consider, honestly, what about your needs is most important to you.

"I think women are completely unaware that they have these expectations for men as partners, or what's more likely is that they feel unreconcilable guilt for the standards they uphold, and anxiety in comparing themselves to the conditions that have to be met by the men they desire. Therefore, they won't admit, or do not come to realize, that this is a source of their own problems and weaknesses in their own existence.

"This is the basic underlying fault of feminism and winning point of the patriarchy. Women's underlying desires uphold the patriarchy." I said to the therapist. "Women do this by making attractive, well off men more desirable and important than anyone else, even themselves. They're all fighting each other to belong with the same small percentage of these men, the patriarch. Women and uneducated feminists use repetitive tropes—that supposedly describe men's behaviours, behaviours that are entirely human and not unique to only men—that are nothing other than distortions used to disguise the fact that the sexual preferences of unintelligent heterosexual women promote the patriarchy. In turn, these distortions end up scapegoating unattractive men, while attractive men are excused. Most women don't realize that for the bulk of our lives, in school, and in search of careers, our success is almost entirely dependent on the opinions of women." I continued to the therapist. I often ranted myself off the deep end in front of her.

Being stuck on a medication that turned me into a chubby loafer in a matter of months coming from the psych ward makes me incompatible to a woman who seeks skinny men more than good character. I consider this an almost universal issue with most women. And I'm including here, men who regularly work out to have an athletic build with less than ten percent body fat, not just men who look malnourished and emaciated.

"There tends to be an exception," I said to the therapist. "If a man is above average height, like six foot three or taller, I've observed that it's more acceptable for those men to be overweight. It seems as though it's acceptable for taller men to be seen with women."

If I was to date a woman who had as much fat on her as those fit men, people would probably start to question if I really like anorexic women. That's right, it's the standard for men to look that way, but if a woman looks like that it's questionable to people, particularly women.

"It's true that there's more overweight and obese men than women. But it's also true that there's more fit and underweight men than women. Why? Because it's a requirement for men. I see it everywhere I go. Just being observant points out the standards there are for men. I see every shape of woman only with skinny and fit men, everywhere I go. Who's in control of that? Women. You'd think that if more men are overweight than women, more women would be with those men. Women get told the standards from TV and movies, and men see it in actuality, in real life, and get shown the standards by the real women they know and see in their own lives.

"Which is worse? *Women don't get rejected.* You take an obese man and an obese woman. The difference there is that the obese woman still gets laid. The obese man will find it difficult to maintain a non-romantic relationship with just one woman." I ranted to the therapist.

It was over with Johanna, she probably thought I had no idea how badly it was over to her, as a result of my wicked complaining, but I really did, because she called it on herself in that she couldn't stroke her ego by objectifying me as well as with her ex-boyfriend. Maybe she thought it would work with me when she moved in, but I had already given up on her when we made out in the starlit lake and she lacked any interest in me romantically after that.

Or maybe she just wanted to be friends, but women really make horrible friends to men because they require you to be around and available for them, but never are available when you need them, even just to suture the loneliness. A friendship with a woman is not much different than having a malicious sister. It's very one sided, all about her, and she makes no effort if what's required is about him.

I hadn't even been too enthralled about Johanna moving in with me in the first place, but she found a room in my house and I had remained nice to her about us soon living together. Although, I really thought she would be infringing on my solace.

Just before my rant about baby mamas, Johanna was pining her ex. He lost $3000 in the Gamestop stock plummet and blamed it on her, so she left him. She says he repeatedly blames her for problems he causes and they have intense arguments in which he calls her useless, spineless, and stupid, among other vicious things. She says she has no other option but to leave when he gets like that. But, she's in love with him.

Johanna drinks a lot more than me, and she had about six tall can empties on the floor in front of her. I had begun quitting drinking so I only drank a couple that night, and I told her I had the perfect song for her, in her case. I listened to her story, like a psychotherapist would do. I asked her questions about the situation to coax out her thoughts and feelings.

"I have the perfect song for you," I said.

I picked up my phone and searched for the song on Spotify. Johanna had been sharing with me her Spotify membership since the summer, when she had just started receiving Covid relief benefits from the government.

"You know how people always say the song that was number one when you were 14 years old is the song that describes you? Well, this song was number one when I turned 14."

"Just listen to the lyrics," I told her.

"I belong a long way from here. Put on a Poncho and played for mosquitos, and drank 'til I was thirsty again. We went searching through thrift store jungles. Found Geronimo's rifle, Marilyn's shampoo and Benny Goodman's corset and pen. Well, okay, I made this up. I promised you I'd never give up. If it makes you happy, it can't be that bad. If it makes you happy, then why the hell are you so sad?" Sheryl Crow sang on my Bluetooth speaker.

"Honestly, Johanna, if you love him, why are you so depressed about him all the time?"

She didn't speak.

"It's just the way she says it too. She was in her early 30s when she released this. You know she's been there. You can tell she really feels it," I explained.

"If it makes you happy, then why the hell are you so *sad?*" Sheryl Crow sang.

I could tell the song hit her right in a tender area. She drooped her head and she was crying. I went to the bathroom. When I came back she was wiping the tears from her eyes.

Sometimes it's best to make someone feel what they feel, even more. It's obviously her choice to feel that way about her boyfriend, so if she wants to feel that way, I want her to really dig in and feel it, like she means it. You'd think that all my thoughts about bad relationships, unresolved feelings about my own physique would make me a bad guy, but it doesn't really. I'm still a pretty good guy when it comes to being in the moment with people. It's just that all those body dysmorphic thoughts I have are indicative of my mental illness. People with schizo-affective disorder usually have symptoms that include delusions: fixed beliefs despite contrary evidence on the subject. My dysmorphia is something I've carried around with me since I was a teenager.

You'd think that I would be perfect for a woman with schizo-affective, or body dysmorphia, but those women usually have the same types of delusions, but with the genders reversed. It makes for a very conflicted dynamic with women who have those delusions.

Little Hollywood, Johanna's sister, has schizo-affective disorder also, and she carries around with her a lot of those body dysmorphic thoughts and anxieties. The trouble I have with her being that way is that she's obese, but wouldn't ever consider dating a man anywhere near as overweight as she is. That tends to be the problem with women's body dysmorphic thoughts. Women rarely hold themselves to the same standards they hold for men.

"There simply aren't enough good looking men to supply all of the women out there. There simply aren't enough sugar daddies to supply all of the sugar babies out there. I'm saying this because I'm genuinely concerned for women's well being. Honestly!" I blurted out to the therapist.

I had been seeing a new therapist since the fall, since around the time Johanna moved in with me. I hadn't any desire to bring up all of these unresolved feelings of insecurity and undesirability from the first therapist, but she coaxed it out of me anyway.

"It's probably not a good idea to go there," I told Anika, the new therapist. "I have a good analogy for it though, which explains why I shouldn't talk about it. You want to hear it?"

"Okay," she said.

"Have you ever read The Alchemist by Paulo Coelho?"

"No. I've heard of it."

"Well, you could say hypothetically, the theme of that book is: love is a mirage. It takes place mostly in a desert. The guy in the book is looking for his destiny. He clearly has intentions to find love or something equally as satiating. But, what exactly is the mirage? Love is a mirage, right? Well, the character in the book meets a woman, in the middle of the desert, in a mirage. But what is the mirage, exactly? Well, in the book, he meets the woman in a mirage in the middle of the desert and finds out, then, that he's right in the middle of a concentration camp in a war. Two opposing forces, right in the middle of the desert, ready to fight at any moment. So, love is a mirage, but you find that when you go looking for it and you find it, it turns out to be a concentration camp where all the hurt, all the oppression is. Maybe it's something you shouldn't go looking for, right?"

"Okay. That's the end of our session. Same time next week?" she said.

I held off as long as I could the ceremonial peeling off of the skin that had scabbed and somewhat healed since seeing that first therapist, but the new therapist slowly took right to looking more closely at the source of the pain in me. She found the wounds with pinpoint precision, almost as if she'd heard it all from some other man before, and before him, and before him.

The psychotherapy with Johanna continued before she left, the last time I saw her.

"He probably gets high when he's around you," I began. "He probably doesn't think clearly because he's manic around you. That's how guys get with women. I get like that. Not with you, but like, Stefi—that's how I was around her. He probably feels like he can do anything and does stupid things like putting $3000 into Gamestop."

"You think so?" she said, timidly, with the glint of a smile forming in her face.
"Ya. It's really typical. He probably really loves you. He probably can't do anything without you."

"He can't," she admitted.

When I came back from the bathroom, after playing the Sheryl Crow for her, I asked her why she doesn't talk to me and is always focused on her cell phone when we drink together. It was a good thing I never really had such a great time drinking with Johanna, because drinking with her that night made me want to get clean again.

"I'm arguing with him," she said.

"If you don't want to see him anymore, why do you even bother? You're just enabling him."

"No, he loves me. I make him manic," she trailed off, crying, realizing I had convinced her and she didn't want to admit I said exactly what she wanted to hear, that she wanted him back despite all the flaws she saw in being with him. It had been as easy as coaxing and manipulating a 23-year-old girl like some kind of scene out of *Lolita*. She wants to be manipulated. They all want and need to be manipulated. The exact reason I wasn't interested in Johanna. The exact reason I loved Mary Oliver and Jennifer Egan.

In Jennifer Egan's collection of short stories, *Emerald City and Other Stories*, all of the stories revolve around very attractive, intelligent female characters who reject all of their suitors. Why? We don't know. But, it still stands that those women in Jennifer Egan's stories appealed to me because they were so headstrong. Egan's stories seem to uphold Simone De Beauvoir's philosophy from *The Second Sex*. Beauvoir writes: "To emancipate woman is to refuse to confine her to the relations she bears to man, not to deny them to her; let her have her independent existence and she will continue nonetheless to exist for him also: mutually recognizing each other as subject, each will yet remain for the other an other."

Still, I haven't *remained* to any woman. Therefore, here I've shared some speculations as to why, some speculations into the details of the ego-love the unenlightened woman searches.

I'm no Satanist, but if you consider sex to be *the Devil* in The Grateful Dead song, *A Friend of the Devil is a Friend of Mine*, you could say that I've been a friend of *the Devil*, and that's the important part, to the right women. I mean, nothing bad has ever happened sexually and I usually like the attitudes of women who believe that *a friend of the Devil is a friend of hers*. There's a lot of women who wouldn't consider that to be a personal philosophy, but there's many more of them who would, and those women, to me, are the best ones. This tends to be a huge difference between men and women. I'm not like that. Rarely will you find men who believe that *a friend of the devil is a friend of his*, although some do. Aside from the fact that at the core, I'm falteringly still in love with a woman who's married, a friend of *the Devil* isn't quite a friend of mine. And really, the best guys to me are only a *friend of the Devil*. I'm no perfect specimen, no man is, but at least I'm still a friend of *the Devil* and it's better than not. It allows willing women to comfortably sleep with me without great alarm or concern.

Johanna and I used to walk together in the fall. We went to a beautiful playground and swung on the swings. "I don't think we'll ever get back together," she said.

"With your ex?"

"Ya."

"You just need to meet someone else. That's how it is: you never really forget someone that meaningful to you until you meet someone else."

"It's just that most guys have ulterior motives."

"Everyone does really. Everyone always considers whether they can make money. It's the one motive that's universal to everyone. Guys just want the other thing, and based on experience with women that have wanted it from me, it's really noticeable when they do. You know why? Because you don't even know what you're asking for. It's different with everyone. It's not like asking for a cookie. Until you're with someone, you have no idea what it is you're asking for. Sex is a completely different thing to everyone. It means something unique to everyone. It's really difficult to make sex a motive because you have no idea what it is you're looking for. This becomes obvious when someone wants something from you but isn't really able to explain what it is they want."

After Johanna moved out, an old Tinder match contacted me unexpectedly and we went on two short dates before St. Patrick's Day. There was nowhere for her to park to come over to my place, so we took a drive in her car. She seemed angry that she couldn't come over without getting herself into a position where she might have to pay a parking fine. She was touching my leg a lot as we talked, parked in the car. Our date wasn't what she expected we would be doing together that night. We had made plans to smoke a joint in my room.

I guess it was because the intentional plans fell through that she became upset. Angered, she made a quick gesture to hit me in the face with her fist a couple of times, but didn't actually hit me. I have very little tolerance for any type of violent act or ideation of violence, so I stopped talking to her and after sitting with her in a parking lot for less than five minutes, she drove me home. Parked outside my building, we were talking again and she was brushing her hand on my leg. When I wasn't looking, she gave me a kiss on the cheek.

It seemed as though in that moment, she was looking for something she didn't really know the meaning of. Sex is a very personal thing to each individual and it's not something you can specifically go looking for. I didn't like the way she approached me to make her move and when I got back home I blocked her from texting me again. I couldn't continue much further with her, to where she thought she was going. Her intentions seemed to be manifesting a little too convoluted for me, and in turn, she somehow felt violent towards me.

Leonard Cohen's *The Stranger Song* translates this truth into a work of art. "Like any dealer he was watching for the card that is so high and wild he'll never need to deal another," Leonard Cohen sang. "He was just some Joseph looking for a manger ... When he talks like this, you don't know what he's after," he continued. And that joker, that Joseph, that man with seemingly no clear motive, that's never been me. It's been women I've known, but never me. It's what that woman parked at the side of my building was after.

I speculate that she was offering a *first time's free* kind of deal, the same way Francine played me. And listening to *The Stranger Song* reminds me of Arthur Nersesian's book *The Fuck-Up* in which a gay man is fucking men and women for a place to live in New York City throughout the book. And at one point near the end of the book there's a typo in which that gay man is described as *her*, and such is the book's fuck-up. I'm guessing it was written this way, about a man, like in Leonard Cohen's song, because women always seem to think it's pathetic to complain about this subject.

I became real life friends with Arthur Nersesian on Facebook in the winter that Johanna left me. He shares interesting pictures of New York City, and he says his IQ is 163.

Johanna and I were together on my birthday in October. I told her that I felt there was no specific pattern defining the types of women I've dated in the past. But after telling her that, I started to ponder: maybe there was a pattern. There seemed to have been no definitive theme relating all the women I've fallen for. I've always been in the happenstance position of being invited to the dance by women. My choice is either yes, or no. I don't really get to pick my dance partners.

A few days later I told Johanna that if I were in my early twenties like her, she would be my world, my *be all end all*, and my life would be complete with her. But she was 22, I had just turned 38, and my position was worlds apart from how I felt at her age, sadly.

"I think my first girlfriend would have stayed with me. That's the sad part. No one else really was very interested in me. But I think *she* would have stayed with me. I feel bad because I didn't really like her. My life would be totally different now if we had stayed together. I probably wouldn't be here with you, and I wouldn't be a writer. My life would just be so much different," I said to Johanna on a walk.

"Would you be happier?"

The thing about my ex-girlfriend (who I was with while I was still deeply in love with seeing Stephanie) was I couldn't morally stay with her much longer than a couple of months. She'd become unreachable for hours, and there'd be some guy parked outside the house. She'd leave without saying hello or goodbye to me, drive away in his car and come back a few minutes later, still not acknowledging me trying to reach her. Eventually she started trying to convince me to do heroin with her because she believed it would make me lose weight. Turns out the kind of guy she was looking for was tall and emaciated, like many women are. But, noting the legendary jazz saxophonist, Charlie Parker, and his ties to heroin, I suspect that junkies aren't always thin.

"I don't think so. I wish it was Francine. Francine was perfect, you know. It's just that she was a thug. She was intelligent, very attractive. Probably the most physically attractive woman I'll ever be with. But she just wanted men to buy her, really. I wish she wasn't like that because otherwise she would have been perfect."

Earlier that day, I thought I saw someone who looked like Francine in a parking lot, which inspired mentioning her to Johanna.

"I don't think she's a thug, she's just a sugar baby," Johanna said.

"Yeah. I guess she is."

We were walking back from the liquor store, about to crack open some beers. We drank until Johanna left to visit her young, very attractive twenty-year-old friend Darlene. Darlene was an out of work construction worker, drank cases of beer every night, and smoked several grams of cannabis every day. I passed out on her couch drinking with her one day. I couldn't really handle alcohol like I once could, and the two of them, Johanna and Darlene, could drink me under the table. And on most occasions with them, they did.

I sent Francine a message around Halloween.

"How about you message me when you pay me that $1000 you owe me," Francine wrote.

"In my books, you're supposed to get something for $1000."

"Fuck off."

"You're a garbage human being."

"You're an arrogant creep. Lose this number."

I drank with Darlene and Johanna on Halloween. I only had one pint the whole night. At the end of the night, Darlene and I had to hold Johanna upright to walk her to the taxi. She passed out in an armchair at Darlene's house.

Darlene, when she drinks, starts talking fast and slurring her words. She sounds like Ozzy Osborne when she starts getting tipsy. I was at her place with her when she was drunk and she had called a drug dealer over and ostensibly told me to wait in her room. I sat in her room watching Sky News but I didn't hear that she told me to wait there. Darlene had spoken garbled nonsense to me, so when I went to find her, the drug dealer she had called over was scared and left immediately after seeing me. Darlene began yelling and screaming at me, stomping on her floor all around the house.

Darlene had assault charges on her for hitting her ex-boyfriend and all of the doors in her house had been kicked open and broken. The paintings on her living room wall had all been knocked down and there were punch holes in the walls. Darlene had been a wreck every time I saw her. I drank coffee most of the times I was with Darlene.

The strange thing is, although I don't see Darlene or talk to her anymore, she had a vintage armchair that looks exactly like an armchair I once owned. She told me she got it from a thrift store nearby. The chair was exactly the same as I had left behind, over 5 years ago, at a room I rented in Darlene's neighbourhood. There was something magic about seeing that chair again. I had so many romantic moments in that chair with Stephanie before she left me and got engaged. Somehow, I've always known I would see that chair again after leaving it behind. I had written my first book sitting in it.

I was a little sad when the Tim Hortons roll up the rim contest ended in April, coinciding with another province-wide Covid lockdown on Easter weekend. I wondered how many of my rock musician friends—and their fan culture that I was connected with on Facebook—would post a picture of Ontario's Premier Photoshopped to look like he was on a PornHub video entitled *Premier Fucks the Entire Province*. There wasn't much else the Premier could do, since most places in Ontario were rolling out the Covid vaccine quite slowly, although, newspapers claimed Canadian's were getting their shots at a rapid pace.

However, I was incredibly saddened when my bicycle was stolen the summer before. I felt lost after it had been stolen from Tim Horton's late one night. It took weeks, after Francine left, to convince Aiden to give it back to me from where he allowed me to store it in his underground parking lot. My bicycle was the only escape from everything pedestrian about my life. There were no rock concerts. Everyone was hibernating. What hurt most was I had bought that bicycle when I was still with Stephanie, the married woman I was still infatuated with. Losing it felt like I was losing my last memory of a woman with whom I felt I experienced the most significant time in my life.

I had nobody to talk to for months before losing my bike,

since Francine left me. Well, there was one other woman. I ran into a woman named Amy that I had first met as an undergrad, who I hadn't talked to in nearly a decade. I was obese when we met, and originally, she had rejected me. We were walking home one night from the bar with her friend, when we were undergrads together. "When was the last time you had sex?" she asked me.

"Four years ago," I said. At that time I had never had sex before.

"I don't know how you can go without it for so long. I had sex with one of my guys yesterday," she said. "I prefer him because of his size," she snickered to her friend.

Then a tall, thin woman, in a tight, short dress, walking down Queen Street, toward us yelled: "I can't get by, these people are taking up the whole street." The two women at my side were both as obese as me. I lost a lot of weight by the time I reconnected with Amy, and so did she.

I reminded Amy that I once knew her, and she was immediately inviting towards me, as I sat near her on the Toronto Transit. She was with a guy I'd never met before. They were flirting, and he was drunkenly going through messages on her phone while she gave me her number. It wasn't long until her arms were flailing in her bed with pillows in her hands, screaming pleasurably, as we made love.

After we finished, she told me, "I drink a twelve pack a day."

She had a few swigs of a 26'er left on her desk, and there were empty Chinese food boxes all over her room. I had no interest in a relationship with her. The first time we finished, she followed me onto the balcony for a cigarette. "I don't think we should go out," she told me.

"No, nothing like that," I said.

She called me on the phone one night asking me to come over

because she said she was raped by a food delivery driver. The night she told me that, we had sex. Then a few weeks later, I was supposed to visit her to console her because she had become disheartened and angered when the fast-food delivery driver *almost* raped her. The night she said that, we had sex again. Then I found out she was in a relationship with the food delivery driver, and she was cheating on him, with me. She was too drunk, every time I saw her, to remember telling me any of those things.

In the depths of summer depression and loneliness, feeling more pedestrian than I had been after my bike was stolen, when I sent Johanna a message I finally felt at home again, and she met me to drink by the lake. We ended our night having a couple of tall cans back downtown. It was the first time I had been drunk in close to a year, and it was the first time I saw Johanna in well over a year, since before I moved to London.

She said she'd pay me back for the drinks, but I wasn't really looking forward to drinking again, even if I liked being with her. Our relationship fit together so nicely, it was as close as I could get to feeling close to Stephanie again, like a surrogate relationship. Johanna and I had a lot to catch up on, but I didn't tell her too much about what had happened in my life while we were separated. We were interrupted by one of the old photographers from O'Reilly's and he ranted, disgruntled, about how bad it is in China, that the Chinese gave us the virus. We talked to him forcing ourselves to be amicable about his political views.

Thankfully, he didn't ask for a beer as the three of us sat on a lifeguard stand at the beach. By the end of the week, Toronto was locked down for the first time that summer, and there were no more bars open. O'Reilly's had already closed it's doors down for good because live music venues hadn't been permitted to open since March, the first spring of the Covid pandemic.

I found out from Johanna that Little Hollywood was living in my housing complex and it just fell into place that Johanna wanted to be close to her sister, subtly mentioning that it would be great to live near me also, and move away from her abusive boyfriend.

Johanna wanted to write more, but hardly did, even though I was supposed to be inspiring those desires in her. As much as I can tell, from living with her, she didn't read much either. She read half of a chapter in a book about improving one's intuition. However, she showed me an old poem of hers one night around Christmas. We were more than halfway through a 40-pack of Budweiser when she handed over her journal to read the poem.

"It could be published," I told her. "I've seen stuff like this in magazines."

"Do you think of me like that?" she asked me, timidly.

"Well, a lot of women are like that," I said. "You can't really tell until you start having sex with them, and then you start to notice."

"I didn't consent the first time I was with my boyfriend," she confided. "That's why I was in the hospital after I met you."

"Well, what happened? Why did you end up with him?"

"I ... just ... ugh," she couldn't explain.

"Do you dislike consenting? A lot of women don't like to. It's usually after you've been together a while, though. Like, it's obvious when a man wants to because if he doesn't, nothing happens. But sometimes women get bored after a while with consenting, they think it ruins the spontaneity," I told her.

"It wasn't like that. Ugh," she sighed.

"Don't feel bad. Don't feel bad if you think you're a masochist. It sounds like you know you are. That's okay. It's a normal thing. A lot of women are. I've been with a lot of women, and a lot of women are. Really. You can't even tell that they are until you start having sex with them. It's not something anyone would ever notice about you," I told her.

Personally, I think of masochism as an undesirable sexual kink. I'm not a sadist and I don't like sadist women either. It's tricky to catch a woman who's not either a sadist or a masochist, I've realized. Sadist women, though, are much more undesirable, in my opinion. They typically don't regard themselves as sadistic, they mistakenly see men as either emasculated by them, or angered. This is because sadist women often don't recognize themselves as sadist, and consider their behaviour to be female empowerment. I just find sadism to be abusive, regardless of what it's considered by women. I've never felt emasculated, I'm certain I'm a man. The whole routine with sadist women always becomes too abusive too quickly for me to get anywhere with one of them. That's probably why I've been with so many masochists in my sex life. I wondered, If the sexual emancipation, and kinkiness of women is so commonplace, could there ever be a woman who wouldn't consider my *vanilla* sexuality so undesirably bathetic.

I had told the new therapist that I often felt undesirable to women, and that I had been unhappy with the frequent alcoholic activity with Johanna. The therapist asked me to make a list of qualities I was looking for in a partner. I think she had expected something in a more positive light, but I thoroughly listed off qualities in women that would make me abscond.

I should probably add a disclaimer here about how my views (as someone reading this may have already realized) don't necessarily reflect every man's opinion. I am a unique individual, although, I believe that being likeable is usually universally likeable to others. In other words, what's likeable to one person, is typically likeable to a lot of people. Some people aren't likeable universally, potentially making them an acquired taste. I'm that uniquely acquired taste kind of person, at least on a romantic level. I think as friends, not many people ever really strongly disliked me.

"She has to respect my emotions," I read the list to the therapist. "She doesn't have a negative opinion of men; isn't trying to hurt others; she's able to have an intellectual conversation; supports my ambitions; not hyper-critical of others, particularly me; able to communicate her emotions without placing blame; uses mostly literal meanings, not word salad; understands her own motivations; doesn't play games; considers what she says and does for how they affect others; can be entertaining, and doesn't always expect to be entertained; sees and expresses the positive character in me; looks for creative musings, and is passionate about arts; shows affection, says I love you, and is comfortable with touching, smiling, and laughing gestures; is open to communicate about our sex life; presents herself respectably in public, and online; is willing to participate in social gatherings in a public manner; doesn't stereotype men; isn't looking for a partner in crime; isn't confined within the realm of female stereotypes; isn't sadistic or masochistic; has a scientific view of spirituality; isn't prudish; likes stories, telling stories and listening to them; isn't an alcoholic or drug addict, and eats healthy; doesn't view sex as a reward, or my primary reason to be in a relationship; and doesn't treat me like a tool." I concluded.

"Obviously, you wouldn't find those problems in everyone," she responded. Anika was definitely more responsive than the first therapist, I was happy that I wasn't expected to rant for 50 minutes anymore.

"No, the problems are different with everyone, but combinations of these characteristics continually appear in every woman

I've tried to be romantic with. Is this exercise supposed to help me build confidence because I said I felt undesirable?" I asked.

"No, I hadn't intended it to build confidence," she said.

"Because it's making me feel like I'm confining myself—because there's no hope of ever finding a girlfriend," I confided.

After Johanna moved back in with her boyfriend, I sent her a message telling her I was lonely.

"You're never going to meet anybody until you get over Stephanie," she wrote.

"It's not about her. I haven't even mentioned her," I said.

"You always tell me you miss her."

"It's stupid, I know. She wasn't even interested in me."

Maybe there had been a tiny glint of a chance for Johanna and me if I hadn't always brought up Stephanie, but I hadn't entirely been interested in Johanna romantically, despite how close we were and how much it felt like home when we were together, especially on occasions when we weren't drinking.

"You're a quality person. You won't have to wait until you're 43 to meet someone significant. You won't be single that long. I know it feels bad right now, but when you meet that right person, it will be amazing!" she said.

I told her about a theory I had discovered based on numerology, which is why Johanna specifically mentioned I'd meet someone before I was 43. My numerology theory was a little kooky, but I do believe in magic, perhaps destiny in this case, and oftentimes the synchronicity of my life, the synchronicity I've fortuitously documented in my books, has been one of the few redeeming features of my life, so, I shed light on my kooky theory with the therapist.

"The calendar years repeat on a consistent pattern," I began to the therapist. "Like, you don't really need to buy a calendar every year because you could buy a finite number of specific years, and you would have every calendar you'd ever need. I haven't figured out what is the least amount of calendars anyone would ever need, but that's not the point of why I'm saying this anyway.

"I met Stephanie in 2014, I was 31, a prime number. The next time that particular year repeats is in 2025, and I will turn 43 that year, another prime number.

"In my first book, by the time our relationship was ending, in 2015, I wrote that it would probably take me 10 years to get over her, which, again, puts me in 2025.

"In my second book I mentioned a strange affinity with Glenn Gould, the Grammy winner who is immortalized as a bronze statue on Front Street. He died the day I was born, at the young age of 50 because doctors prescribed him all kinds of pharmaceuticals for his mental illness, and he also predicted, accurately, the year of his death based on numerology.

"But also, there's a song by Hayden called, Bad as They Seem, in which he's in a relationship with a woman who's 16, it was useless to love her because she was so young, and he says he'll be living with his parents for free until he's 43. Like me living off disability for free right now. But the other thing about it is, Stephanie would have been perfect for me when I was still a musician, when I was 25, but she's almost 10 years younger and she would have only been 16 years old. I could have used her at 25. I was so depressed. But, by the time I met her at 31, I was starting to become a writer, and as I wrote that first book about the relationship we were having together, the magic that happened between us, I gradually became a writer, growing apart from the musician I once was, the musician that would have loved her perfectly.

"She came into my life too late. Or I came into her life too late. But, it still stands that I don't think, based on this numerology, based on the magic evidently between Stephanie and me, that

I'll meet anyone significant until I'm 43," I explained.

"Is it comforting for you to think that," she asked.

"Yeah. It is, kinda."

"Why is that?"

"Because I can focus on other things. Maybe discovering this theory should tell me that maybe a relationship isn't really something I need right now. Like how last week you challenged my need to be in a relationship. Like, maybe I would be best to focus on something else."

"So, what would you focus on instead?"

"Writing. Getting somewhere with my writing. Having a career as a writer."

"Have you thought of getting your work published, instead of self-publishing?" she asked.

"Yes, I've been thinking about it. I think with a better publisher I'd have a much better chance at success," I said.

The thing about my numerology theory is that a symptom of my illness is magical thinking. Seeing life as magical that way is sometimes considered by psychology as delusional thinking. I had grown into deliberately looking out for magic, since I had twice been able to work the happenings in my life into books of magical realism. Life had broke out of the norm to give me a sign, and this numerology was another magical breakthrough in my mind, no matter how delusional.

As April was approaching nothing magical had happened in quite a long while, but I had a lot of time. If anything magical were to happen, I believed it wouldn't be romance.

I had started talking to Eileen over text messages for the first time since we broke up. I guess I told her that I really liked her one night as we were messaging each other.

"I really like you too. I like your energy," she wrote. "But I'm just working on myself right now."

I supposed she had said that because she might have thought I was coming on to her and wasn't interested in me romantically anymore.

"I'm not looking for a relationship with anyone anymore. I've been hurt too much," I admitted.

Then I again explained my numerology theory, this time to Eileen over text messages.

"I think we carry a part of each of our past loves with us forever. It's our experiences that shape us for our future," she said.

I concluded by sending her a link to the Hayden song, *Bad as They Seem,* and explained the significance to me, as it pertained to my numerology.

"I love how music can do that," she concluded.

Earlier in the week had been sort of another bit of the world opening my life up to magic, but for the first time in my life the magic seemed to have opened up to conspire against me, like the magic of meeting your true love, but also losing her in one fell swoop.

That is to say, in happenstance, I stood outside the Tim Horton's by my building having a cigarette and a guy rode into the parking lot on my bike that had been stolen in the previous summer. Of all the places to be standing, on any day, in the middle of millions of people throughout the entire city, there was my bike, right in front of me. I felt as though the guy riding it was coming back like a sea turtle to its place of birth.

He looked around. I could tell he was looking for a place to put down the bike before going inside the store. I smoked my cigarette, looking casual, as if I didn't see him there. Then he put the bike down and went inside. I moved over to the bike, picked it up, and was about to ride away when he quickly came at me and grabbed me. I pushed him off and yelled, "It's my bike!" He backed off and I rode away.

Looking into his eyes before riding off with the bike was intense. That moment when I saw my bike there, reclaiming it, was intense. I couldn't believe it. I had my bike back, and was riding it. *What a miracle,* I thought.

My life that had been excessively pedestrian suddenly turned into the most exhilarating joyride through the busy April streets of thousands of cars and millions of people travelling in every direction, and getting to where they needed to be. In that moment, it had been a stroke of perfectly timed synchronicity that put me back on the streets, cycling with the traffic.

I rode my bike, and rode, through the streets, hardly paying attention to anywhere I went. I continued to ride, and felt ecstatic, completely joyous, filled with the wondrous feeling of magical intervention because I had been standing exactly where I needed to stand to ride my bike again. I couldn't believe my luck at that very moment. I felt, in that moment, as though everything was perfect and I could trust life completely.

Once I arrived back at home, I thought of Mary Oliver, how she wrote in her book called *Felicity,* "Love is the one thing the heart craves and love is the one thing you can't steal."

I lay in bed and the words of Mary Oliver echoed in my heart, as I reread her book, *Felicity,* thinking of how fitting everything had been that day.

BUT WHAT OF THE MAGIC of that day, anyway? Was there magic in the world opening up to conspire the theft and assault charges when I walked back to Tim Hortons later on in the night?

"But it's my bike!" I pleaded to one of the officers.

"Do you have any evidence?" he asked.

I couldn't sleep that night. I was manic depressed. Eluding the last gyzym of consciousness was truly the only magic remaining in the day's rivulets. I was at least mad to live. Beat there, like brethren, elated, yet hell-bent.

I felt anxious, so the only thing I could think of to calm my nerves—to do the last thing that made me happy that night—to reread Mary Oliver's *Felicity*. The best I could get from it the second time was that I was still alive, still breathing, no matter the tossing and turning in bed, insomnious. "The point is, you're you, and that's for keeps," Mary Oliver had written.

THE THING ABOUT MEETING STEPHANIE on Vimy Ridge Day in 2014 is that when I first moved to Toronto, I lived in Mimico, less than a block from the Vimy Ridge War Memorial on Lakeshore Drive. I never actually went in that park because it always looked so cold. Still, even after I think about the numerology based on the undeniable love I felt for Stephanie, I haven't been to the Vimy Ridge War Memorial park, and have no plans to.

But, as everything closed down because of Covid when I was seeing Amy, who I so happened to fuck on Vimy Ridge Day, just after things ended with Francine, I hardly went anywhere. I shopped at Wal-Mart. If I felt like walking, or I had no money for the subway, I'd walk up Runnymede to the Wal-Mart, or if I had money for the subway, I could get to the Wal-Mart on Bloor. Circle K stopped stocking the two-dollar cookies that I liked so I started eating salami sandwiches on miniature naan breads that came in a package of about 20.

As I got chubbier, and was being urged to stay inside by the provincial government, I worried about the calories I was eating every time I made a sandwich out of two miniature naans. But after Johanna left, I wasn't drinking anymore, so I became a little leaner. The winter waned into spring warmth and I felt comfortable going outside for long walks, on my usual route, with no one to see, or into High Park to look at the faces, or sometimes I walked at great length and found myself resting in parks I couldn't identify by name.

I sometimes found myself lost, walking, but everything I looked at was interesting. Of all the places I've ever been, or remember visiting, Toronto is by far the most interesting place to look at. I've been to Vancouver and Chicago as a teenager, but I don't remember much about my times there, anymore.

I sometimes made a point out of nostalgia to go back to Mimico to the Valu-Mart where I always used to buy my groceries when I first moved to Toronto. I looked at my old apartment, and wondered if the Filipino family that lived in the apartment on the top floor still lived there. Surely the little teenaged girl was already all grown up, and likely already finished University. She had left about a dozen pairs of tiny little panties in my closet before I moved in. I didn't mention it to her and the pairs of panties remained in the same place in the closet until my last memories of living there.

I shopped at the Valu-Mart in Mimico in the winter, around the time Johanna was moving back in with her boyfriend, and I ran into Liz, the pretty blonde that was at O'Reilly's when I had interviewed Guerin Tracy. I hardly recognized Liz with her mask on, near the seafood counter. Her eyes lit up, and I assumed she was smiling behind her mask, but I smiled when I saw her, and she waved me over to talk to her. She asked me to stop by her cheese shop when I could. They were still doing curb-side pickups outside the store. I told her that I always wanted to go to a fancy cheese shop in Kensington Market.

"Do you still talk to Martin?" she asked.

"I designed his new book that he released in the fall." I said. "Johanna says he's in a bit of legal trouble though. I don't know much about it and it's none of my business anyway."

Martin French was accused of assaulting Karen outside his apartment, both him and Karen were totally drugged out. I found out the crown was seeking three months time as a plea bargain. As much as I liked Martin, he had been funding a lot of his ventures in the music business by illegally dealing pharmaceuticals. He was pretty deep into the cocaine scene also, and Johanna says Shell always had a problem with his drug problems.

"I jammed with Guerin a bit in the fall," I said.

"How was that?" Liz asked.

"We mostly drank. I think he lost interest when he found out I wasn't taking it too seriously, so we just started drinking. I didn't really want to drink the whole time so we only got together three times and then the whole thing went bust."

"Oh, that's too bad. I hear Nerds are breaking up. Did you hear anything about that?" she said.

"I heard all about it from Guerin when we were jamming."

"Am I going to see a story for the magazine about it? Did Martin end the magazine?"

"Good question. I don't really know. I should write a story though. I might talk to Ted about an interview. Everyone says Wes is a bit of a control freak, so Ted seems like the guy to talk to. He's like second in command at Nerds camp."

"Good plan."

"Well, the smell, of ... what is that, squid? That smell is getting to me."

"Could be squid. Okay, well, come into the shop," she said.

When I talked to Martin again, I found out the magazine was caput, but I ran into Ted on my route anyway. He and Megan had started a dog walking service, so he had a bunch of dogs he was looking after, out on the balcony when he called at me. He came downstairs and sat on the step with me.

"Pop a squat," Ted said to me, and I sat down beside him. "What's going on man? How's it going?" he asked.

"Not too bad. Just out for a walk," I told him.

"So, Nerds broke up. I guess you heard."

"Yeah, Guerin told me. We were jamming a bit in the fall. He said there was some kind of conflict with Wes."

Guerin actually told me that they broke up because Ted never practiced his guitar parts, and wasn't interested in playing in the band anymore because he wanted to become a family man with Megan. Guerin and I both agreed that it was admirable of Ted to want that with Megan.

"Ya, Wes didn't like Megan," Ted told me.

"What's wrong with Megan?"

"Don't tell anyone this, but a couple times Megan hit me when she was drunk. I've never hit her, but she hit me a few times. She was drunk. Wes didn't like that we stayed together after. I'm in love with her, what can I say?"

"Well, Wes isn't in control of you. He sounds like he wants to control everything. Everyone says he's a bit of a control freak."

"He really is. You know, and I did a lot for that band. Megan did a lot for us. She drove us to a lot of our gigs, with all our equipment in her car" Ted explained.

"None of you guys drive, I guess."

"No, and Megan and I did all kinds of promotions for the band. Wes takes credit for everything. He uses the band to get business doing marketing for companies. So all those ads you'd see on T.V. and promos on the radio: he used all that stuff to get more business for himself."

"It seems like Wes wanted to do marketing more than he really wanted to do music."

"Yeah, and Aiden, Guerin and I wrote most of the new stuff we were going to release. You know who wrote all those last few singles? Me," Ted said.

"Oh, I didn't know that. So, what are you going to do now?"

"Well, Megan just took a job, and we started the dog care business and I help her with that. Aiden's back doing the teaching. I'd like to start teaching again."

"What's Aiden doing these days?"

"He's still around. Obviously, doing the teaching, but he's still chopping too."

"Is that illegal now?"

"Oh, it's totally illegal. It's even more illegal now that you can get it from licensed dealers."

"Well, does it bring in much money?" I asked.

"It's pretty decent," he said.

The conversation took a turn that most certainly couldn't be published in a *Smash* interview. Ted had already suggested everything was off the record when he mentioned I shouldn't say anything about Megan hitting him in the past. I mentioned the story about taking my bike back and being charged. It seemed that people were mostly of the opinion that taking a bike that belongs to you isn't illegal. I just had to prove it first.

I slowly gathered pictures I had of the bike before it had been stolen from me. I printed them at Wal-Mart, and connected the pictures in a binder with the digital versions of the pictures on a memory card so that the police could examine the digital timestamp on them. I took my time preparing everything to bring to the police. In compiling the evidence, I hoped that the crown would be able to drop the charges or at least allow me to plead to a mischief charge. Even the cop, when he drove me home to pick up the bike as evidence, told me that I wouldn't serve any time. "You'll get a slap on the wrist," the officer said.

Eileen told me she thought everything would be okay with my legal trouble, that I wouldn't serve time, and talking to her after the arrest had been the most comforting thing to me. We made plans to go for a walk together, but she was always busy baking and taking care of her kids. With no intention of starting a relationship, she seemed to lack enthusiasm in continuing our relationship beyond text messages. But, that was fine with me, because when I felt alone I sent messages to Eileen, and she always responded seemingly in a good mood. Even when we were romantic, becoming closer, as in the beginnings of a romantic relationship, she had always been very sweet to me.

She told me that after we broke up she got into a relationship with a guy, moved into a house with him and after a while, something happened causing the guy to have to be physically removed from the house. Eileen didn't tell me the details of what happened, but she ended up moving into a woman's shelter for a short time with her children. She seems to be doing better now, living in an apartment that is partly provided by social assistance.

Amy also ended up in a woman's shelter after committing suicide in her housing unit and disturbing her roommates. Shortly after, she found herself in a tiny home in a small town outside Toronto. She had asked me to keep some of her things in storage for her while she went away, but I declined. I suppose that's why she stopped talking to me. It was impossible for me to take her seriously anyway. She was hung up on her two children already out of her custody because of her reckless alcohol addiction. She had no money to support them without custody of them, and because Amy was gone, her family almost forgot about her completely. It was difficult for me to spend time with Amy because of psychopathic, suicidal, drunken outbursts, and the denial that alcohol was feeding her into a downward spiral of mental illness.

Everyone living on the margins had been tied to the whipping post by the Covid pandemic. I did what I could to keep a healthy mind. When I visited the psychiatrist to have my injection he said, "Everything will be back to normal probably by August." The beginning of April, when I was arrested, was a stressfully long time to wait until my first court date, let alone being forced into hibernation for a another summer.

"I haven't bought your books," the psychiatrist said. "But I'm going to."

"Well, someone bought them. They aren't bestsellers or anything, but I'm competing against every favourite author I have," I told him.

"So, how are you doing?" he asked.

"I see those flyers all around the hospital. Apparently, the doctors and nurses are going to be charged with malfeasance and war crimes for administering the vaccines."

"Are you worried about that?"

"Not really. You all had them, right? I mean, it's kind of silly."

"I had it," the doctor said. "I didn't grow a second head."

I laughed.

"I'm not sure why people do that. Bunch of fear mongers."

"I think they just want to stir things up."

"Yeah, I guess there's nothing else to do."

"So, I'm going to buy your book right now," he said, and left me with the nurse to administer my Paliperidone injection.

"Right arm today," the nurse said.

The thing about the fear of it all had been getting to me when I read Margaret Atwood's story, *The Age of Lead,* about Jane and Vincent, a couple that had known each other since a young age. The couple, Atwood's story says, finally had sex in their thirties and they didn't quite hit it off in bed, which was fitting to me, since I can't say I really hit it off with any women either. Atwood writes, in the story: "He couldn't take it seriously, and accused her of being too solemn about it. She thought he might be gay, but was afraid to ask him; she dreaded feeling irrelevant to him, excluded."

But what scared me is, Margaret's story says: "A week before Vincent's forty-third birthday, Jane went to see him in the hospital ... He was in for a mutated virus that didn't even have a name yet ... He was in for the duration."

I started to think that my *age 43* numerology might actually be my curtain call and, contemplating my own mortality, I cried about Jane's old friend, Vincent, dying just prior to 43, in Atwood's story. The magic of my life and everything that was magical about my relationship with the estranged love of my life had begun to turn sour, had turned into a delusion. If the sexton is going to pull the curtain on me at 43, surely all the magic of the theatrics of my life would have to be delusional. *Life is just a series of twisting, turning, winding delusions.*

IN THE FIRST SUMMER OF the Covid outbreak, I reconnected with a woman I met in my first Fine Arts master's degree program. She was getting married when we met at the university, but she gave me a hand written card that she designed. The inscription was meant to be cheerful. I found out when we reconnected that she had a crush on me. Obviously, because she had been engaged to be married, nothing ever blossomed between us, but as she started up with me again, she was single again, and she coaxed me to flirt with her a bit and I took a liking to it, at first.

We took a drive in her convertible after her work at the design studio one night. "I'm at the point in my life where I'm looking for a relationship," I told her. This made her feel like I was asking her to be in a relationship, she told me after. I was simply asserting that I wasn't looking for a fling.

"I wish it wasn't ending now. I still want to be with you," I said as she was dropping me off.

"What, were you expecting to get laid?" she asked.

I was speechless. It's like she didn't hear a thing I said to her. We sat silent for a moment.

"Do I kiss you?" I asked, as she was parked in my lot, dropping me off from our date.

"I don't know, do you?" she said, sarcastically.

I kissed her on the lips quickly and said goodbye.

After that she continued to be critical of me every time I flirted with her in text messages. I wasn't sure why she had went to the trouble to coax me into flirting with her in the first place if she would be angered by it once our relationship was becoming a reality.

"You're giving me mixed signals," I wrote. "Look at what you're saying to me, you're being hyper-critical."

"I don't tell this to many people," she began. "I have herpes. Don't tell anyone about that."

"Do you want to talk about it?"

She didn't respond for a few hours, but she concluded that she wasn't interested to talk about it. We wrote to each other in text messages for about a month after that, but she was standoffish for the duration. I thought about being with her, but the thought that sex isn't particularly enjoyable for me without the added displeasure of contracting HPV, it seemed useless to pursue her for anything more than a friendship. But, because she was so standoffish, it was impossible for me to see her as a friend either. She was always in a bad mood, and I tried to console her and be comforting to her, but if I was ever feeling down she didn't care at all. The relationship was very one-sided, where I was a participant, and she was doing the bare minimum to appease me. This is typically the way it goes with women who say they want to be friends, and it's discomforting, and usually useless.

When I had been friends with Stephanie, she didn't act like that. She was incredibly responsive to me, to the point that I felt she was interested in me romantically. Most of the times we were together, we were getting drunk and in high spirits. We fed off each other's energy, but neither of us were emotionally draining to the other. My sister says that when you're having fun drinking, the good spirits prevents you from gaining so much weight, but after she was gone, I just gained weight until I left Johanna the first time, hailing my old drunken feelings of being with Stephanie.

In the second summer of the Covid outbreak, as spring recently turned to summer, I saw couples carousing on the streets and I remembered the old days, being with Stephanie, and how somehow, I had become a sober adult. Soberly, I pined for those old times because I felt monotonous in staying clean, like nothing romantic would ever happen sober. I did my best to remain steadfast about having no desire for a romantic relationship.

I'm happier single, I said to myself.

Having a muse would be the most satisfying, and the only women I ever really found to satisfy me as muses, were the women I read in books.

"Who are your influences?" the therapist asked me. "I know you said Kerouac before."

"Well, I'm reading this," and I showed her a copy of *The Journals of Anaïs Nin*.

"I've heard of Nin," she said.

"I think I'm influenced by her. I read one of her books when I was writing my first book. I always read Henry Miller when I was writing my books, for inspiration."

"What about Bukowski?"

"People told me my first book was a little like Bukowski, but I don't think I'm really like that. I hadn't read any Bukowski before I wrote my first book, so it couldn't have been influenced by him. I don't aspire to live a life like him. He was a very detestable person, and hated everyone," I responded.

"Well, I guess if you have a pessimistic view of relationships, you get compared to that."

"I think it's more like Nin. I'm influenced by Henry Miller and Kerouac because they had lives and relationships I admire, but I don't sound like them. As far as putting a sentence together, and turn of phrase goes, it's a lot more like Nin."

The thing that seems to separate me from Bukowski, seems to be a similarity I share with Henry Miller, which is described by Anaïs Nin in her journals. She writes: "His life has been one long opposition to will, he was born passive. It is a philosophy created out of temperament. He has practiced letting things happen. Now he wants to express in literature the effectiveness of relaxing the will for the sake of enjoyment. He is the man who dodged jobs, responsibilities, ties. He freed himself of all tasks but one; to write, perhaps at the expense of smaller men and lesser artists."

This similarity to Henry Miller seemed to define my attitude towards writing, and the mentality of his work that influenced my writing. The fact that Nin was a crucial muse to Miller for such a fecund time in his writing, is testament to the greatness I still recognize in her, her greatness as a muse, even lasting until the moments of writing my own manifestations and reflections.

In thinking of this, I couldn't long for anyone I've ever known, because I haven't known anyone so influential to that degree.

"You're stuck in the past," the therapist told me, weeks later.

"I don't think I'm stuck in the past, really," I said.

I hadn't been. The only thing that I longed for from the past was the dissipated potential that becomes evident early on in the progressions of relationships with women. After that, it becomes difficult to see much potential when you realize they haven't chosen you as their partner, and they want you as a muse. And, I've been just that. A muse. A good one, to a lot of women and men.

But perhaps I'm asking a lot. Perhaps I'm asking too much. Perhaps that moment when a muse inspires the fecund moments progressing into creation is just a flash of light, nothing more than a blink. That's what it is sometimes, and even Kerouac described the sensation as a *Tic*. The only bit of me living in the past was the aftertaste, the afterimage of the creations, the manifestations that came out of me completed and once inspired by the blinks of moments with muses, whoever—whatever—they were.

I looked out my window after my therapy that day and I saw a woman who became apparent to me across the lane behind my building shortly after I moved there. I wondered if it was her that inspired my new story, or Francine. She certainly looked similar to Francine, and every time I saw that woman who looked like Francine, I was reminded that the characters I wrote about were like recreated, hand-drawn versions of the persons they actually were, including myself, like an ersatz light used to see those characters through my eyes.

The prose read:

The New Window

Like the end of December, especially during the hours of sidereal visions, April was another month affording letters to myself—salty-eyed stealing of someone else's idea of what's expected of a man, a lover; the type that's the antithesis of a *would-be* father figure. Yet, here I lay like a ledger in the red; in the black just a nick late to afford a place with Fran, but *in* the nick to look through the glass at the-new-pretty-in-pink-tights exhibit welcoming the first light of May, outside the new suite. Unaware of her exhibition, black khaki clothed a twisting wrist and hand, nicked hip high under loose drawstring.

Cinco de Mayo, there she was in the window again, yelling at her sister ... about the fallen toaster, the mishandled, bagged ego-purchases of exorbitant yoga and bonfire attire to be, or maybe a *has been* dad bod. In any case of going concern there she was again, Dutch-faced and vintage blonde, as I read and reread Joan's translator notes about the intricacies of *Dasein* in Heidegger's middle-aged quandary with being and time.

Looking back and again out the window, feeling darkened by the second row of Mansard roofs a lane away, my body was meditative and mind only physical. As a first splash of morning light glared through my thick white blinds, opened at half-mast, my mind emerged meditative and my body was soon physical.
Longing for the scent of Francine's morning java, and blonde hair spared at my side before moving to embrace her, I looked out my window for someone, something other than the echoes of potentially deal-breaking snoring.   In the pickup line for coffee, she looked quite younger than in the place where—unknow-

ingly to her—Us had been entwined, where the glassy-lit exhibit greets her porch; where I felt I knew her, and, yet unquestioned, she had known me.

But that's it!

I knew too much about a woman on the other side of the lane, a spitting image of Francine—oversaturated myself with too much of her in my mind. Stood beside her, I housed no suite of new meditations, only the new window's refractions of specious memories of what had been home.

Perhaps there could be another time, but is there to be another light?

fin

So, I sent out stories and poems to magazines, still worried about my legal troubles, if I would be incarcerated at some point, but I had to be myself in continuing on, humanly. Although I may appear to be sketched out in some places, in so much as my entire life existing on paper—which all seems like a delusion—it all seems too real, all at the same time. The reality of it too wild to communicate and express at times, and with due space and time to become a little more nonchalant about things, to elude the wilderness of it all, the inexpressible gradually turns to sketches that seem realistic. Such is like the water cycle of that world I live, like streams and wastewater, and precipitation. I watched the rain of spring come down, and I had little to write because the wilderness of it all had been too grey to be describable in words.

I felt as though somewhere in there, everything became a delusion, a long string of delusions, and the future seemed to be much of the same. *The future is distorted.* In as much as I can analyze the distortions of the rock music in the backgrounds of life's moments, they just play out now part and parcel of a hope in hell.

Johanna took me to her boyfriend's place in the winter before my legal troubles, where I met him for the first time. He had his own legal troubles the spring after that, as well. He hadn't been paying his rent, as some kind of gesture of anti-establishment ideology. He was going to court on internet video sessions and had delayed his proceedings because he was allowed to wait until traditional court proceedings were back underway, therefore delaying anymore rent payments for his apartment.

Johanna's boyfriend seemed manic when I met him. He never stopped walking around his house talking incessantly, and Johanna sat with me on his couch, with her hand on my leg. I had told her that I used to love when Eileen touched me, that she used to touch me when we were dating, and that no other woman really ever touched me like Eileen. So, that night Johanna started touching me more, and I felt more comfortable amid her boyfriend's confusion and mania.

I became wary of him and wanted to leave soon after arriving at his apartment, but he suggested I take one of his favourite books home with me. He likely wanted me to have it because he thought of me as some kind of famous writer. That's how he treated me.

"It's this book he loves, about how to pick up women," Johanna told me, as her boyfriend searched his apartment for the book.

"I don't think I'd like that. I think it would just anger me."

"Just take it. It would mean a lot to him."

Her boyfriend placed the book on my lap.

"I don't think I want this," I told him.

"I insist. It's a gift."

"Just take it," Johanna said.

He drove us home, and I was expecting Johanna to come with me, but when I was about to get out of the car, Johanna dropped her boyfriend's book on my lap, told me to take it, and stayed in the car to head back to her boyfriend's apartment. It became clear to me where the importance in her life was leaning. After that moment, I hardly wanted to be Johanna's friend anymore. The relationship with her seemed to be mostly trouble for me. I guess they wanted me to take the book because I repeatedly told Johanna that I was lonely. I certainly was.

Eileen had been consistently replying to my messages, I went to the Valu-Mart in Mimico and spent almost the last of my disability money on some vegetables. I made a decision to quit eating meat again, because despite being more mobile as the weather was becoming warmer everyday, I felt my meat intake was preventing me from dropping some of the extra weight I had gained over the winter months.

I had twenty dollars left and I felt I needed some kind of company, with someone who I thought might surprise me, so I decided I would pay Liz a visit at the cheese shop. I remembered her asking me to visit her when we spoke near the seafood counter at the Valu-Mart.

It was about a 45-minute ride, either by bus and subway, or taking the 501 streetcar downtown and walking into Kensington Market, but it wasn't too far away from my building in Bloor West. The first thing that caught my eye was the streetcar so I hopped on the back without paying the fare. I regularly did this and had no troubles since the Toronto Transit recently replaced their older streetcars with long accordion style cars that had more entrances in the back half.

I arrived in Kensington Market, and I walked around. I wasn't quite sure where Liz worked. All of the stores had signs noting that they would admit orders for curbside pickup, but as far as the name of the cheese shop where she worked, I only vaguely knew the name of the store. I finally found it after walking, at length, around Kensington Market, a couple of times walking around the same block.

There was a man standing outside the door, and I could see Liz inside in an apron at the counter.

"Are you waiting," I asked the man.

He turned to me and when I saw his face I recognized him from somewhere, but I wasn't sure where.

"They're preparing my order," he said. "You can get something when they bring mine."

I waited there, and I thought of where I had seen him before. I soon realized I knew the man's name, but had never actually talked to him before. He was a musician. He wasn't a famous musician or anything, just a local jazz musician who I'd seen play at The Rex Hotel before. Actually, I never saw him play much but he was there at a very strange moment when I walked in the doors and I was anxious and had still been off of my medication for over a year.

The day I moved back from London, before I went into the hospital, I was dropped off my bus on University Avenue just a couple of blocks away from The Rex. I had no plans to go anywhere that day, and oddly enough, I wasn't worried about having no money either. As I said, I've never really worried about money. Although, I only had fifty cents in my pocket. I walked down Queen Street and as I approached The Rex, I heard a jazz band in the middle of a tune, a saxophonist blowing a solo. I stepped in the door. It was still the dinner set, so there was no cover to get in. Obviously, I hadn't enough money to stay as a customer.

Those were good times when the live music in the restaurants was swinging, and there was some great music happening on stage. As I stood at the cheese shop, those days seemed so far gone.

The trumpeter looked at me as he was standing off the stage, near the door and I reached into my pocket, pulled out my last fifty cents and dropped it into the tip jar at the stage. The trumpeter smiled at me and nodded. I looked at the musicians, listened for a minute. It was hip, and I turned to the trumpeter, and said, "Thank you." Then I walked away, out the door. I actually had no place to go.

I later did a little researching to find out about the band playing that night. I found out the trumpeter's name, and checked out some of his recordings on Spotify.

That same trumpeter was waiting for his order at Liz's cheese shop in Kensington Market with me. I thought of that moment, walking into The Rex and dropping in the very last of my money, with nowhere to go, just arriving in Toronto from London. Heck, you can't really buy anything for fifty cents, so I figured supporting the music I love would be the best way to use that little bit of money.

And as I stood there, outside the cheese shop, I looked in at Liz, preparing everything for his order, I realized that buying a big block of cheese wasn't the best thing I could do with the last of my money. I didn't even know if I had enough money, with twenty dollars, to buy anything. It was possible that the cheese there was terribly expensive, I haven't ever bought cheese, and I wasn't really sure.

"Oh, she's coming now," he said to me, as Liz walked towards the door holding his bag of cheese.

I decided I would leave. I knew I could do better with the last of my money, even if I needed a little inspiration that day from a great musical artist like Liz. I thought of listening to Liz's music as I walked home, but I didn't. I don't think she saw that I was there, but I was happy that I had changed my mind.

I turned on Nerds' first album, listening through my earbuds, back on my route, this time in the middle of the day, the sky clear and blue. I made my way through the streets of cars in traffic, and through the streets between the tall buildings downtown, which eventually became shorter buildings and houses as I came closer to High Park.

It was the same as ever, or at least the same as it had been for some time, just a tiny blip where I lost myself and left normalcy behind. I found myself back in Toronto listening to Nerds again. I was able to walk through the park, look at the streams, and geese, and the people walking their dogs on and off leashes. I listened to the songs that I had inspired Wes to write, initially, when they were first starting out.

I had twenty dollars in my pocket.

The album came to a close, and I listened to it again. Their first album wasn't long enough to last the entire walk from Kensington Market, wander around High Park and back into Bloor West, so I listened to it over and over. I walked into the Circle K convenience store to pour myself a coffee. I paid and walked home, listening to Nerds again.

Other Books From Bolero Bird

Naive Melody: The Early Novellas of Michael Whone (2025)

Mind the Bits: Notes of a Schizophrenic - Michael Whone (2025)

little bit die - Jason Emde (2023)